DAT

RAISE F

· N U M 8 E R S ·
1NF1N1TY

"From its poignant beginning to its heart-stopping conclusion, *Infinity* will thrill readers new to the *Numbers* series as well as fans of the two previous titles. Told alternately in the distinctive voices of Adam and Sarah, the novel gives readers a remarkably original premise, authentic world-building, and genuinely creepy villains."
— *VOYA*

"The action never stops in this dystopian trilogy conclusion. Readers will be caught up in the multiple mysteries as well as the couple's emotional turmoil."
— *School Library Journal*

"A tense, action-filled narrative told through alternating voices, amping up the drama and the stakes of the mind-bending story. This finale satisfies."
— *Booklist*

"A little violent, a little supernatural, a little mysterious, a lot sentimental; fans of the trilogy won't be disappointed as this story edges toward magical thriller."
— *Kirkus Reviews*

· NUM8ERS ·
1NF1N1TY

RACHEL WARD

Chicken House

SCHOLASTIC INC.

No part of this publication may be reproduced, stored in a retrieval system, or transmitted in any form or by any means, electronic, mechanical, photocopying, recording, or otherwise, without written permission of the publisher. For information regarding permission, write to Scholastic Inc., Attention: Permissions Department, 557 Broadway, New York, NY 10012.

All rights reserved. Published by Scholastic Inc. Originally published in hardcover in 2012 by Chicken House, an imprint of Scholastic Inc. SCHOLASTIC, CHICKEN HOUSE, and associated logos are trademarks and/or registered trademarks of Scholastic Inc.

JUL 16 2013   www.scholastic.com

ISBN 978-0-545-38191-8

12 11 10 9 8 7 6 5 4 3 2 1   13 14 15 16 17 18/0

Printed in the U.S.A.   40
First Scholastic paperback printing, July 2013

The text type was set in Dante, Gothic 720 BT, and Memento.
The display type was set in Trade Gothic Extended.

Book design by Christopher Stengel

THIS IS FOR MY PARENTS,
SHIRLEY AND DAVID,
AND GRANDPARENTS AND
THOSE WHO WENT BEFORE . . .
AND FOR ALI AND PETE AND
WHOEVER FOLLOWS AFTERWARD.
AND FOR OZZY, OF COURSE.

DRAGONS IN THE FOREST

The little girl sits in the dirt. She's been exploring the forest, but now her legs are tired and she doesn't want to walk anymore. Anyway, it's nice here. With all the stones and leaves and twigs around her, she could make a nest for birds, or a house for mice. Her fingers are busy—picking things up, putting them down, arranging them—and her mind's busy, too. She makes marks in the dirt with a stick—lines and circles—and her mouth moves as she sings herself the song that goes with her dust-pictures.

She hears the motorbikes before she sees them, a background whine that becomes a drone that turns into a roar. She holds her hands over her ears. She's never seen a motorbike before and now there are three, big and black and fast, belching out trails of dark smoke. The girl glimpses metal and rubber and leather between the trees.

"Dragons," she whispers, and the pupils in her blue eyes grow wide.

The motorbikes slow down. They stop. They're growling softly now, not roaring, but they're too near. The girl sits very still. She can see them. Can they see her? The dragon at the front takes off part of its head. There's a man inside. He scans the trees on either side of the road that cuts through the forest.

For a moment their eyes meet.

The man's face is pale, but his colors are dark, like his clothes and his dragon. A swirl of gray and purple and black. The girl doesn't like the colors. She's never seen people-colors like these before. And she doesn't like him looking at her. His eyes are dark, almost black, and they are hurting her.

She closes her own eyes quickly, and buries her face in her knees.

"Seen something, boss?"

"Just a kid. Let's go." His voice is hard and low.

The dragons' growl turns into a roar again, and then they're gone.

The girl squints through her eyelashes. There's nothing to show the dragons were ever there apart from a cloud of dust, which hangs in the air and then settles. Slowly she unwinds and leans forward, gathering in an armful of twigs and leaves, destroying her dust-pictures. If there are dragons here, she will need to build a big nest to keep the birds and the mice safe. Better make it big enough to keep *her* safe, too. She piles more and more stuff around her, snuggles in, and closes her eyes. Then she waits for the dreams to come—the colors and pictures that will send her to sleep.

She wakes when she hears someone shouting her name.

"Mia! Mii-aa! Where are you? Mii-aa!"

She doesn't move. She wants to see if her nest is a good one, if she can be found. She loves playing hide-and-seek.

"Mia! Mii-aa! Where are you? Where are you?"

The voice is getting closer. The girl curls in a tight little ball and buries her face in her knees again. It's fun, this game.

She hears footsteps crunching through the undergrowth. Closer, closer, closer . . .

"Mia! There you are!"

Feet are right next to the nest. Mia turns her head a little and peeks upward. The woman looks cross. The skin is creased between her blue eyes. Mia doesn't like it. She wants her to be smiling and laughing. But her colors are the same as always, a haze of blue and lilac around her, colors that mean one thing—Mummy.

Mia turns her head into her knees again. She doesn't want Mummy to shout at her.

Sarah bends down and grabs her daughter under her armpits. She lifts her up, still curled tightly in a ball, and holds her close.

"Mia," she says, "you must stay where I can see you. Are you listening?"

Mia puts her thumb in her mouth.

"I was just worried. I thought . . . I thought I'd lost you. I'm not cross."

Mia takes her thumb out of her mouth and looks up. Then she reaches forward to wrap her arms round her mummy. Everything's OK—there won't be shouting and tears this time.

"Dragons," she says. "Me see dragons."

Sarah looks toward the road. She heard motorcycles a few minutes ago. "Do you mean motorbikes?" she says, hugging her daughter close. She starts walking away from the road and back into the forest.

"Dragons," says Mia. "Noisy."

"Did you see wolves and bears as well?" Sarah says, smiling.

Mia shakes her head.

"Dragons," she says again, firmly this time.

"Better get back to the camp, then. The dragons won't come near our fire. We'll be safe there."

But Mia doesn't feel safe, even now, holding on to Mummy.

The dragons she saw made smoke themselves. A fire wouldn't frighten them away, she thinks. They'd *like* a fire.

Better to hide. Better to make a nest and hide from the man with the dark colors all around him.

ADAM

"I know you."

I've watched the guy moving closer, picking his way through the ragged group of tents and shelters.

Here we go again, I think. It's the same everywhere. That's why I try and keep away from people. But that's dangerous, too, 'cause you're vulnerable on your own. We ain't got nothing valuable, but people'll still rob you, take what little you got—food, clothes, even firewood. It's happened too many times now. We have to stay near others. *"Safety in numbers,"* Sarah says.

Ignore him and he might go away.

I keep my head down, bashing the tent peg into the hard ground with a rock.

Just a few feet away, he crouches down beside me, leaning forward to get a look at my face.

"I know you," he says again. "You're Adam Dawson."

I twist away. My fingers tighten around the rock.

He reaches across and touches my sleeve. He's too close. I can see the dirt under his fingernails, the bits of sawdust in his straggly beard.

"Adam," he says, smiling. He's tipping his face, trying to get me to make eye contact. "Adam, you saved my life."

My heart's thudding in my chest. I can't deal with this. I want him to go away.

"No, mate," I say, and my voice goes all croaky. "You got the wrong bloke."

"No, I've seen you. I'll never forget you, your . . . face."

He means my scars, my burned skin.

"You saved me, Adam. I was in London. My flat was in the basement, right by the river. I saw you on the telly and I got out. So did millions of others. You're a hero."

Same story. I've heard it over and over.

I was only on the telly once, but it was the last TV most people saw. There are no TVs or computers in England now, no screens or phones. The networks and transmitters never got put back after the quake, at the beginning of the Chaos. And so I'm stuck in everyone's memories as that mad-eyed, scar-faced boy, staring into a TV camera and shouting the odds about the end of the world. And they remember me because I was right. The world did come to an end—the world as we knew it, anyway.

Now everyone I talk to treats me like some sort of celebrity, some sort of savior. I don't want it.

"We've got some meat," the man continues, when it's clear I'm not going to talk. "Venison. Someone shot a deer, a big one. Come and join us. Come and eat with us."

I stop bashing the tent peg. Meat . . . Can't remember the last time we ate meat. It's gotta be better than the nettle soup we were going to have. I look over toward Sarah and Mia, to Sarah's brothers. Marty and Luke are scuffing the leaves on the ground, looking for dry twigs, anything that would do for kindling. Mia's sitting in our handbarrow, watching as Sarah unrolls the mats we use for beds. She's tiny for a child who's two. Her arms and legs are as thin and tawny as the twigs the boys are looking for. She's almost like a little doll, with that mass of tight blonde curls, full lips, and eyes that don't miss a thing.

Sarah's pretending to be busy, but I know she's watching me out of the corner of her eye, waiting for my reaction. I know she's heard every word. She don't say nothing. She don't need to. She's hungry; we all are. My mouth floods with saliva at the thought of a square meal. But I know what's gonna come with it—the fuss, the backslapping, the questions.

I can't stand people looking at me, and I can't stand looking at them, seeing their numbers. . . .

Everyone, everywhere has a number—the day they're gonna die. I hate that I can see these numbers. I hate the feelings that come with them. Sometimes I could grab a flaming stick out of the middle of the fire and plunge it into my own eyes to stop me seeing. Stop me feeling the suffering and pain that's waiting for every single person I meet. I've been scarred by fire, it's nearly killed me twice, but maybe it would take away the thing that hurts me most.

The only thing preventing me is Sarah. I can't do that to her. I'm difficult enough as it is, moody, restless. I couldn't expect her to stay with me if I was blind as well.

She looks straight at me then, with those blue eyes of hers, and her number speaks to me, brings me the comfort and the warmth it always does—an ending full of light and love. 07252075. The promise that we'll be together, me and her, fifty years from now, when she passes from this life, easy as if she was slipping into a warm bath.

Sarah.

I turn back to the stranger crouching next to me, and I force myself to nod at him and smile.

"We will join you. Thanks," I say. The words sound like someone else's.

His face lights up. "Great. Cool. Come over anytime. We're in the bender farthest from the path." He points to a tunnel-shaped tent, pitched between two tree trunks. "I'm Daniel, by the way. It's good to meet you, Adam. I've waited a long time for this." As he strides off, I hear him calling, "Carrie, he's here. He's really here. . . ."

There's anxiety bubbling up inside me. It was a mistake to say yes. I'm already regretting it. I raise my arm up and smash the rock down on the hook of the tent peg so heavily that the peg bends and I scrape my knuckles on the ground.

"Aargh! Fff . . . ow!" I'm trying not to swear in front of the kids. It's fucking difficult sometimes. I drop the rock, brush the worst of the dirt off my fingers, and put them in my mouth, sucking hard to take the pain away. It don't work. And it don't take the anxiety away, neither, or the anger. Nothing does.

Sarah comes nearer. "Thank you," she says.

I shrug, still sucking at my knuckles. I'm glad I've got my mouth full. It stops me saying what I want to say. *I don't want to be around people, Sarah. They're all the same. I can't handle it.*

"Hurt, did it?" she says.

I take my hand away from my mouth and inspect it.

"Be alright in a minute. Just took the skin off."

She digs in one of our bags on the barrow and pulls out a tube of antiseptic cream. The end's been rolled over and over, to squeeze out every last bit. There's not much left.

"Don't waste it on me."

"Shh."

She puts a tiny bit on the end of her finger and dots it onto my scrapes, then gently rubs it in. It's so intimate — her finger-tip touching my skin lightly, only a few cells making contact. I feel my body relaxing, the anger dying away.

Me and her. It's all I've ever wanted. Even after everything we've been through — the quake, the Chaos, the fire, the gypsy life, looking after Mia and Marty and Luke — we're still together. I stare at her finger. And at this moment I'd give anything for the rest of the world to go away. I want to be alone with her, my arms around her and our faces close.

I hold her hands in both of mine. "Sarah, let's go," I beg. "Let's go somewhere else." I hate myself for sounding so desperate.

She presses her lips together, pulls her hands away. The moment's gone.

"We've just got here, Adam. We're staying."

And so we stay.

• • •

We sit on logs around Daniel's fire. His venison stew's pretty watery, but it's so long since we had something like this that it's almost overwhelming.

Marty and Luke wolf it down so the gravy dribbles down their chins. They wipe at it and lick their fingers, laughing. No one tells them to behave. It's good to see them filling their bellies, their faces glowing with the warmth of it. They're good boys. The fire that killed my nan took their mum and dad, too. They were so quiet at first, with a haunted look in their eyes all the time. They hated being outside, didn't know what to do with theirselves, cut off from their Xboxes and flat-screen TVs. But we've learnt stuff together: how to set a trap for a rabbit, how to make a fire. I've never had brothers or sisters before.

Mia sits on Sarah's lap, her wide eyes looking at all the faces lit up by the fire: Daniel, his partner Carrie, their neighbors. It's like she's trying to remember them.

I eat slowly, savoring each mouthful, trying to concentrate on the food, not the conversation. The backslapping and the fuss is over, and I'm waiting for the questions. The others are talking about the things people always talk about these days: food, water, fuel, cold, hunger, illness. Especially illness. It bothers me, can't pretend it don't. We struggle to find food, to keep warm, and we manage. But if one of us gets ill, what do we do?

The boys have both got good numbers—11212088 and

09032092 — but numbers can change. Mia showed me that, the night of the fire, the night of the quake. She's got Nan's number now. It freaks me out when I catch it in her eyes. She's got a smoker's death, gasping for breath. It fitted right with Nan — it seems cruel now it belongs to Mia.

I don't know the rules anymore.

"It's not so bad here," someone says. "Dan's a doctor."

I look at Daniel. Dirty beard, long hair tied back in a pony-tail, yellow fingernails. He don't look like a doctor.

"Used to be." He shrugs. "I worked in a hospital in London, before it was trashed by looters after the Chaos." He shakes his head. "You'd have thought people would respect hospitals, wouldn't you? But we became targets, raided for drugs, supplies, metal to melt down. I left after the Battle of St. Thomas's in March 2028. Four hundred people killed, most of my friends gone. The police, the army, the government — they all abandoned us. Where were they? Where the hell were they?" He pauses for a moment. His hands are clenched in his lap, the sinews taut like wires from his fingers to his wrists. Then he takes a deep breath. "So what brings you here?" he says, turning it back to me.

First question. Everyone's quiet, waiting for my answer.

"We're just keeping our heads down, moving around," I say, looking at the floor.

"You heading somewhere in particular?"

"Just away. From London, from the big cities. Too many people, too dangerous."

"There are people looking for you, you know. They've been here, asking."

I stop chewing and look up. "People? Who?"

Daniel shakes his head. "They didn't give names. Three of them, on motorbikes. The sort of people you don't grass to. No one said a word."

He puts a hand on my shoulder. He's trying to be reassuring, but contact like that makes me edgy. Besides, the only people who can still get gas are the so-called government, or the gangs that have taken over the cities.

I was under arrest when the quake struck, charged with a murder I never done. The government had it in for me, tried to silence me. I assumed my criminal record would have been wiped in the Chaos. But maybe not. The thought makes my blood run cold.

If it's the government looking, I definitely don't want to be found. I got nothing to say to them or their spooks, and I won't be banged up in a cell again. *I can't be.* I don't want nothing to do with gangs, neither, the armed thugs who own the cities now. Another reason to clear out, stay in the country.

"When?" My throat's gone dry. It's all I can do to get the word out.

"This morning. We had a drone up here, too." He grins. "Shot it out of the sky."

"I heard bikes this afternoon when I was looking for Mia," Sarah says to me quietly.

I jump to my feet. "Shit, we gotta get out of here."

Sarah frowns. "Not now, Adam. Not in the dark."

"Didn't you hear what he just said?"

She shakes her head. "It's *dark*. And we're all tired."

"We're going in the morning, then," I say. "First light." I sit down again, slowly, but I can't eat no more. The stew is sitting in my stomach like a stone. I can't keep still. My legs are jiggling, ready to run.

The buzz of conversation starts up again. "We can't keep on the move forever," Sarah says under her breath. "We've been at it for two years, Adam, and I can't walk miles anymore."

I look at her swelling belly. We don't know exactly how far gone she is but it must be seven or eight months.

"And what about my brothers?" she says. "Mia? They need to live somewhere. They need a home. We all do."

Home. I had a home once. Seems like years ago, but it stopped being home once Mum died. And I had another one, with Nan, 'cept I never realized what I'd got 'til it had gone and so had she.

"Home's not a place, Sarah, it's people. We got all we need with us."

"We need *more* people," she says. "I'm going to have a baby, if you hadn't noticed. I had Mia on my own, on a grotty bathroom floor in the squat, and I want this to be different. Daniel's a doctor. We have to stay here. And we can't run faster than motorbikes. If they want to find us, they will."

She don't get it. Even after all this time, she don't

understand how bad it is to be handcuffed, thrown in a cell, completely powerless.

"I'm not going to be found, Sarah. No one's going to take me away from you and lock me up again. No one!"

I'm shouting now. Everyone around the fire falls silent, looking at me or looking away.

"All right," she says, keeping her voice low. "We'll talk about it later."

I take no notice of her and plow on. "Think about what staying means. I'm not being paranoid. There are people after me."

"Yeah, after *you*."

So that's it. Her words sting like a slap on the face.

People begin to gather up their bowls and drift away.

"Come on, boys," Daniel says to Marty and Luke. "I'll take you back to your tent."

The boys trudge off. The laughter and the warmth of the meal's gone from their faces. Marty looks worried.

Then it's just Sarah and me and Mia by the fire. "Do you want me to go?" I say.

Her eyes flick up to mine and then away. "We can't keep running like this, Adam."

"Do you want me to leave you here?" I say.

"Mummy Daddy cross?" Mia says in a little voice. Her eyes are fixed on us, missing nothing.

"I'm not cross," Sarah says quickly. I force a smile at Mia, but I know she's not buying it.

"I'm chipped," I say, trying to carry on the argument.

"Mia's chipped. That drone could've picked us up and sent our location back to wherever, whoever, it came from. Even if it didn't, I'm so bloody recognizable." Almost without thinking I put my hand up to my scarred skin. "If we stay it'll only be days before they find us. Maybe hours. And then what?"

"We don't even know what they want, Adam. They might want to shake you by the hand and thank you. Perhaps you saved them, too."

There's something about the way she says it, an edge. Like she's mocking me. I can't stand it. My hand finds a piece of wood, and I launch it into the fire with such force that sparks fly up. Sarah flinches and Mia jumps, but it don't stop me. I pick up another log and do the same.

"I didn't ask for this, Sarah. I didn't ask for none of this. I never wanted to see numbers. I never wanted all this death in my head, all this pain."

Mia's eyes are filling with tears, and Sarah's not looking at me. I know I'm ranting, but I can't stop.

"I'm seventeen, with a girlfriend and three children to look after, a baby on the way, and no home and no food, and it's *never gonna get better.* All I know is it's gonna end one day because I see the end everywhere, in everyone, and I wish I didn't. And even that isn't certain because it could all *change.* It could all be over tomorrow, or the next day, or the next. Do you think I want this?"

"Do you think any of us want this?" she says.

And now my stomach's churning. If she's not on my side no more, then I got nothing.

But we have to go. It's not safe here.

SARAH

Adam shakes my shoulder before it's even light. He's a dark shape next to me. I can't see his features. Even inside the tent, the cold air is nipping at my face.

"Sarah," he whispers. "It's time to get up. We have to go."

I pull my sleeping bag up around my ears and turn my back to him.

"*Sarah*," he hisses. "It's time."

I take a deep breath in, and then push the air out—slowly, slowly, slowly. I'm scared of what I'm going to do next, but I'm doing it, anyway.

"I'm not leaving."

"What?"

"I'm not leaving."

"Yeah, you are. We're packing up this morning. Like I said. Moving on."

I wriggle around so I'm facing him again. My heart's thumping.

"I don't want to go. I want to stay here for the winter.

They're nice people. There's a doctor and there's food. Adam, please."

"Sarah —"

"No. I'm going back to sleep."

But I don't. The blood's beating in my ears, and I lie there listening to Adam's silence. *Have I done the right thing?* But my swelling ankles tell me it's right. And my blistered hands tell me it's right. And the gentle snoring of the kids tells me that we all need a rest. It's time to stop moving and just be a family for a while. Me, Adam, Marty, Luke, Mia — and the new baby.

It's a funny sort of family. I can't ever be the boys' proper mum — I'll always be their sister — but I'm the only relative they've got left, so I'm the nearest thing to a mum they're going to have now. And Adam's not anyone's father, though Mia calls him Daddy. When she said it to him that first time — *"Da da da da"* — his face changed. It was like the sun coming out. We were dog-tired, sitting by the side of the road, hadn't even put a tent up, but Mia was wide awake.

"Did you hear what she said? Did you hear, Sarah?"

She did it again, *"Dada,"* and reached her arms up toward him. He scooped her up and danced around with her, and it was like he'd forgotten everything else, just for a minute. It reminded me why I loved him.

Love him, I remind myself now. *Love, not loved. I love Adam Dawson.*

If I say it often enough, think it often enough, perhaps I'll still believe it.

But it's difficult if you know that when he looks in your eyes he can see you dying.

I close my eyes and try to empty my head of it all, to let sleep wash over me and blank me out, but everything's all mixed up: people, places, words, and numbers.

Always numbers.

. . .

Mia's the last to wake, which is unusual. When she eventually crawls out of the tent, Marty and Luke have already left to forage in the forest. Her eyes are pink and glassy, and her cheeks are flushed.

"Me poorly," she whispers.

I swoop down next to her and put my hand on her forehead. She's red-hot. Her nose is blocked up and she's breathing through her mouth. Her breath is sour and sickly.

"Adam, she's burning up."

"Shit."

This is the thing we dread: Mia getting a temperature.

The night of the quake—in the heat of the fire—she had some kind of fit. I can still see her twitching in Adam's arms, outside the burning house, her legs and arms all stiff. That's when her number changed. She was meant to die that day—but Adam got her out and Val, his nan, died in the fire instead. Their numbers swapped. Their fates swapped. I don't know how it happened.

Will it happen now if her temperature gets too high?

"Daniel," Adam says. "I'll get Daniel."

It's only a couple of minutes until Daniel comes, but it feels like hours.

"Let's have a look," he says as he crawls into the tent. He pulls out a stethoscope from his rucksack and listens to her chest. "Not too bad," he says. He takes her temperature. "Nearly a hundred and one. Let's give her some acetaminophen."

"Have you got some?" Our last supplies ran out months ago.

Daniel produces a full bottle from one of the rucksack pockets. I look at it, then at him. Where did he get a full bottle of medicine? We check every empty house and shop, and sometimes we're lucky enough to find a sachet. But a full bottle . . .

"I've got quite a bit of . . . kit," he mutters sheepishly.

"How? Where from?"

He smiles. "The government's got a stash. You just need to know how to get at it."

"And you do?"

"I've got contacts, shall we say."

"Government ones?"

He smiles again but doesn't say anything more.

"Looks like a virus," he says. "Keep her drinking and I'll give her acetaminophen every four hours." He crawls out again.

Adam looks in.

"He's got medicine, Adam," I say. "He's got a whole bag of tricks."

"I know."

"So this is a good place to stay."

He sighs. "We don't have much choice."

I know it's a big deal for him.

"Thank you," I say.

"Just don't blame me if . . ."

"If what?"

"I dunno. If it all goes wrong. I feel . . ." He struggles to find the words. "Like a sitting duck," he says finally.

"It'll be all right. We'll be all right." I really want to believe it.

"Maybe," he says, but he doesn't sound convinced. "I'm going to start a fire."

I turn back to Mia. She's calmer already.

Her trusting eyes fix on mine and her number fills my head. I don't see numbers, like Adam, but I know hers. Adam told me. 02202054. Twenty-five years left. It's better than the lifespan she started with, but it's not enough. I feel sick at the thought. My daughter can't die at twenty-seven; it's too young.

She needs to find another number, a better number.

Could I give her mine, like Val did? But how? How did she do it? If it would help her, I'd give it to her, of course I would. I'd give my life for Mia.

Her hair is damp from her sweat, darker and curlier than ever, but still blonde. It's like a halo. All I can think is that twenty-five years is nothing. It'll be over in the blink of an eye.

I gather her into my arms. Tears stream down my cheeks.

Mia puts her clammy hand up to my face.

"Don't, Mummy. Mummy sad?"

I don't want to upset her but I can't stop crying.

I wish I didn't know. Adam's brought this gift, this curse, into our lives. It's not his fault, but right now, at this moment, I resent him for it. I hate him.

It's not natural to know this stuff.

It crushes you.

ADAM

I hear Sarah sobbing as I make the fire. Should I go back in the tent? I wait outside for a moment, listening, then I walk away into the forest.

I can't blame her for being scared. I've been scared myself for most of my life, ever since I realized what the numbers meant. I was only five. That's a long time.

She's frightened for Mia, and so am I. But I'm frightened *of* her, too. I'm ashamed, but I can't help it.

It's wrong, isn't it? She's a beautiful child—with those blue eyes, that blonde hair, her skin all tanned from living outdoors. A golden child. People look at her wherever we go—after they've clocked me first. And of course it's not her looks that freak me out, it's her number. She don't have the number she was born with. I get this spooky feeling when I look in her eyes.

Her number sort of shimmers in my head, like it's not there. It reminds me every time of Nan and that terrible day in the fire, at the start of the Chaos.

Nan wasn't meant to die that day. She had twenty-seven years left. I always thought she'd be there for me, that I could rely on her. I thought she was safe. But she weren't. She died. There one minute, gone the next. I can't even think about it now without getting a lump in my throat. *It's not fair.* None of this is fair. I didn't want Mia to die, so I walked into the fire to save her. But I didn't want Nan to die, neither. I can't help wondering: Did Mia take Nan's number? Was it murder? Or did Nan give it to her?

No one knows what happened. It's our secret—mine and Sarah's—and I reckon it should stay that way.

And this feeling about Mia, I've never even told Sarah. But what happened that night of the fire wasn't right.

It wasn't natural.

I don't know what the rules are anymore. I don't know how it all works. If Mia can change things to save herself, does someone else always have to pay the price?

•   •   •

In the evening, we gather together around Daniel's fire again.

It's rabbit stew this time. The hot food's intoxicating, it makes me warm and woozy. Marty and Luke caught the rabbits—they're feeling proud, I can tell. They're pushing each other, and laughing and joking. Someone starts singing, an old song.

Mia's gazing into the fire and the flames cast a rosy light on her face. She looks more like an angel than ever. She seems better. Daniel's acetaminophen did the trick. But what about next time? Sarah's right—we do need people.

I put my arm around Sarah and rest my hand on her waist. Beneath my fingers I can feel the baby moving. She leans into me. I kiss the top of her head, close my eyes, and breathe in, listening to the singing. For a moment, just a split second, I'm happy. We were right to stay.

The noise of the engines is so quiet at first I hardly notice it. It's like it's part of the singing, and then, as it gets louder, everyone hears it at the same time and the singing stops.

The light from the flames flickers on our silent faces. Then I realize everyone's looking at me.

"They're back," Daniel says. He don't need to say who.

"Three of them, on motorbikes. The sort of people you don't grass to."

I jump to my feet, grab the boys' hands.

"Come on," I say. "Let's go. Now."

Marty and Luke look at Sarah. She puts her hand up to my wrist, trying to stop me.

"Adam . . ."

It's no good. I know it's not logical, but I've got to move.

"Please," I say.

She sees the look on my face and struggles up, with Mia in her arms.

"Adam, stay put. We're all here for you," Daniel says. He

looks around the circle and everyone nods in agreement. He's speaking for all of them. But I can't just sit still. I can't.

We stumble away from the fire, picking our way between shelters and out into the dark forest where we huddle together, facing the camp. We can see here, but not be seen. The sound of the bikes has stopped, but now there are three points of light bobbing toward the fire. Soon I can see three figures moving: men in black leather jackets and trousers, black boots, black gauntlets. They sweep the beams of their flashlights to either side as they approach, and stop just outside the circle. There's an obvious gap in the places we've left—why did no one think to close it up?

Every eye's on the men. It's not just their clothes that make them different, it's the way they carry theirselves, and their weapons: army-issue rifles slung over their shoulders and a belt of ammo across their chests.

The man in the middle steps forward. He's got gray hair, cut short, and a strong jaw, almost square. His face is pale, like he hasn't been outside for a while, but I couldn't say how old he is. Thirty? Sixty?

"We don't want to break up the party," he says. His voice is deep but sharp, clipped. "Just looking for somewhere to stay the night."

Sounds innocent enough. Three travelers in need of some sleep.

Next to me, Mia whimpers.

The boys are quiet, watching like us.

Sarah shushes Mia, who's curled up in her arms, hiding her face in her hands. "Dragons," she's whispering. "Noisy dragons."

"Ssh, Mia, shh." The warm, relaxed feeling we had around the fire is long gone. Sarah's face is pinched and anxious.

"You're welcome to stay," Daniel says. "We'll find you some food, too, something hot."

The three of them step closer to the fire and take up our places in the circle, with their backs to us. The man who spoke is obviously the leader. To his left there's a smaller guy, wiry and mean-looking. The other one is huge, a mountain of a man with long dark hair.

It's cold now that we're beyond the reach of the fire. Marty and Luke are shivering. Mia starts to cough. Sarah holds her in closer, but nothing can muffle the noise completely.

There's no reaction from the people by the fire. Everyone faces the flames in silence. Then the questions start.

"You know who we're looking for," says the man with gray hair. "Have you seen him? Have you seen Adam Dawson?"

I hold my breath.

Will Daniel and the others lie? Will they save us, or will they save their own skins?

"I've seen him, yes," says Daniel. "He passed this way, but he's gone now."

Not a lie, strictly speaking. But not a giveaway, neither.

"How long?"

"He left just after lunch."

"So you won't mind if we search the camp?"

"Do you have a warrant?"

The man laughs. It's a grating sound, like he doesn't use it often. "No, I don't have a warrant. I don't need one. I'm on government business. My name's Saul, that's all you need to know."

So it *is* the government. I feel the world crashing in on me. Is it the old murder charge? Is that why they're here?

Daniel's looking uncomfortable now, but he's still civil.

"You want to search in the dark?"

"That's right."

Daniel shrugs. "We've got nothing to hide here, but these are our homes. There are babies asleep. It's getting late now. Why not wait until morning?"

Saul pauses. "We could—I suppose. After all, no one will go far in this darkness, will they?"

Daniel don't answer the question. He says, "Do you have a tent?"

"We do, but you're right, brother, it's getting late. We'll just bed down in our sleeping bags near the fire."

Daniel nods, but Saul wasn't asking permission.

The evening's over. People start making their way back to their shelters. The three strangers walk away into the darkness to fetch their things.

"What do we do now?" Sarah whispers.

"We get our stuff and go," I say.

"But it's pitch-black out here. How far do you think we'll get?"

"I don't know. We just need somewhere to hide."

"In the dark?"

Why doesn't she understand? Why isn't she scared of these men? Why can't she just agree with me for once? Mia starts coughing again.

"Stop coughing, Mia. I need to think."

"It's not her fault. Look, they're coming back. Shh, Mia, shh." Sarah unbuttons her coat and wraps it around Mia, rocking her back and forth.

"Away," says Mia softly. "Man go away."

We watch as the three men put their sleeping bags on the ground near the fire. They have a bottle, too. The gold liquid catches the light of the fire as they pass it between them. Everyone else has gone now.

They talk quietly among themselves, matey, jokey, like men used to spending time together. My body jerks as a shiver runs down my spine. It's perishing cold. How long before they go to sleep and we can tiptoe away? The bottle's nearly empty, the fire's starting to die down.

Then, without turning around, the man with the gray hair, Saul, raises his voice and calls out into the night air, "Why don't you come nearer to the fire, Adam? You must be freezing out there."

•   •   •

It feels like we're cornered, though there aren't any walls behind us, just miles and miles of dark, empty forest. He must have heard Mia coughing. At least I don't need to argue with Adam anymore.

"Help me up," I say to Adam, and we all shuffle forward.

Marty and Luke are hiding behind me.

The three men turn to watch us. I'm not scared at first, but as we get closer to the fire, and to the men looking at us, I get the creeps. I can feel the leader's dark eyes on me. It's as if he's touching me, and I want to slap him away.

Mia starts to cry. I wrap my coat farther around her, but she's cowering inside, burrowing her head under my armpit, and her thin little body is racked with tears and coughs. "Away," she keeps saying through her tears. "Man go away."

"How did you know we were there?" Adam asks.

Saul switches his attention away from me, and I realize I've been holding my breath.

"I could sense you."

And just for a moment I believe him — he's a devil, a vampire, a werewolf. Someone, something, with superhuman powers.

Then he laughs. "I picked up your chip in my beam." He pats the flashlight hanging off his belt. "It's a clever little thing, this. And I heard the child coughing," he adds. "She sounds bad."

"She's fine," I say, "but I need to get her into bed now."

"Is this your daughter?" Saul says. He's not talking to me

but to Adam, who neither agrees nor puts him straight. "Let me look at her."

"No," I say, holding Mia closer, shielding her, but Saul's on his feet and reaching toward me before I know it. He grabs my lapel and peels the front of my coat back. And now his fingers are touching her face, turning her head toward him, his thumb prying open her eyelid.

"What are you —? Stop it!"

"Mum-my!" Mia sobs.

Her frightened blue eye stares up at him, then her chest heaves, her arms and legs shoot out, and she starts to kick and yell. I've never seen her react like this to anyone.

"Get off her!" Adam and I are both shouting now.

Saul doesn't apologize, just steps away. But he carries on staring at her, and then he laughs again, that harsh, unnatural sound.

"The girl in the woods," he says. "She's a noisy one. Looks like an angel but screams like a devil."

I hate him. I hate this man, who thinks nothing of hurting a child and laughs when she cries. I can't believe he touched her. It makes me feel sick.

"She's frightened. You frightened her," I say, trying to shush Mia. "Come on, Adam, let's go."

But Adam's not moving.

"I'll be there in a minute," he says. His voice sounds strange, forced.

"Adam?"

But he's looking at Saul like the rest of the world doesn't exist. Like I don't exist.

I leave him there.

. . .

Marty and Luke fall asleep instantly but it takes me ages to settle Mia down again.

"No like man," she hiccups between sobs.

"I don't, either," I say, stroking her hair. "Don't worry about him now. It's sleep time."

"Mummy sing 'Twinkle'?"

"Twinkle, Twinkle, Little Star." It's her favorite. Mia loves stars. That's one thing we gained from the Chaos—deep, black night skies, studded with stars, planets, and constellations, shooting stars, and a moon that's as familiar to us as the sun.

I start to sing softly, trying not to wake my brothers.

Mia stretches her arms above her. She opens and closes her hands, making them twinkle.

After a while she puts her thumb in her mouth and turns onto her side. I tuck a blanket around her, then I slip out of the tent and sit outside to wait for Adam.

ADAM

We stand six feet apart, looking at each other. There's a white scar above his left eye.

I'm nearly shitting myself, but I don't want him to know how scared I am. I make myself stand square, look him right in the eyes. And when I do, his number blows me away. It's something else.

02162029.

But it's not the date that's getting to me.

It's the death itself.

It's extraordinary, a split second of pain and despair and rage and panic. I've never felt anything like it. I can't explain, except it feels like death from the outside in, every surface screaming, with scraping, gnawing, piercing pain all over his body, and death from the inside out, every cell collapsing, all coming together in a white point of agony.

I want to look away, to break away from his pain, but there's something else. His number shimmers in my head. The more I try and get a fix on it, the more it dances in and out of focus, light and dark all mixed up. There one minute, gone the next.

The whole thing—the death, the shimmering—makes me feel dizzy. The ground's shifting underneath my feet.

"Adam," Saul says. "Sit down. Have a drink."

"Thanks," I say, "but I don't. Drink. That stuff."

I do sit down, though. Ain't got much choice—my legs have turned to jelly.

Saul nods at the other two men, and they melt away into the darkness.

"You took some finding," Saul says. He sits down next to me, reaches out for the whiskey bottle, and swigs the dregs.

I'm concentrating on my breathing, trying to control the panic that's washing through me.

Who is this man? What sort of death could feel like that?

"Why were you looking?" I say, my voice higher than I want it to be. "What do you want me for?"

"I've come to take you away from all this."

It's like there's a hand clutching at my throat. I told Sarah. I *told* her. They're after me and they want to take me away.

"Take me? Where? Why?"

"We work for the government. We're putting this country back on track. We need people like you, Adam. Strong people. People who can lead. *Gifted* people."

That throws me.

"Gifted," I say, trying out the word for size. Nobody's ever called me *gifted* before. "But the government don't want to know," I say. "I tried to tell them two years ago and they tried to shut me up, to silence me."

"They arrested you."

"Yeah."

"For murder."

"But I didn't do it! I was being framed. I didn't kill nobody."

I'm properly scared now. Whoever this guy is, whatever he is, he knows a lot about me. Too much.

"That was then. Things are different now. We want your help."

"What help could I be now? I already told everyone the end was coming—and it came."

"But it's not the end, Adam," he explains. "It's the start, the start of a new world where people like you are listened to, respected, valued. You can make a difference."

I don't know what to say. "What do you mean?"

"People listened to you before. They started getting out of London. They'll listen to you again. You can be a figurehead. Where you see danger, you can warn people—get them away from areas that are going to flood, out of buildings that are going to collapse. You can get children to feeding stations. You can help, Adam. You can help us rebuild this country."

I don't believe him. Why would the people that tried to silence me before want my help now?

"It took you long enough to find me. I'm chipped. You could've picked me up anytime you liked."

"We've been putting the information infrastructure back together. The software, the systems. We had the drones but we couldn't communicate with them. We can now. We've got phones, too—a basic network up and running again. We're piecing things back together, back how they used to be, but we need people like you."

"I want to help people, of course I do, but —"

"You don't have to live like this," he carries on as if I hadn't said anything. "You don't have to live the way this lot do, sitting in the dirt like savages. Your kids don't have to go hungry or cold. They don't have to be ill."

"What d'you mean?"

"There are places with electricity, heat, food, medicine."

"In England?"

"England, Scotland, Wales. There are pockets of civilization left. Enclaves. For the ones who can *contribute*."

"Cities?"

He shrugs. "Parts of cities, some buildings, country estates, farms. Places that thought ahead. Planned. Wind turbines, solid fuel burners, solar panels. Some of them survived intact. Others have been repaired."

He smiles and throws his empty bottle into the fire.

"It's going to be a hard winter, Adam. Hardest since 2010."

I know he's right. There are at least three people in the camp who won't make it to the spring. I think of Marty and Luke and Mia and Sarah, of the last two years just getting by.

Pockets of civilization.

The thought of being indoors, warm and dry, is almost painful.

"What would I have to do?"

Saul claps me on the back like it's a done deal.

"Play your part, my friend. Play your part. We're laying the foundations for a different society, where intuition and science work hand in hand. The old ways and the new. People who are special, people like you, who've been misunderstood, we want to understand you."

Gifted. Misunderstood. Understand.

I know he's choosing his words carefully, spinning them. I can feel he's stringing me along and I don't like it. But they're warm words. They make me feel warm.

"Talk to Sarah about it," he says, all calm. "Talk to her now. Come back and tell me what she says."

"She's probably asleep by now. I don't want to wake her."

"So talk to her first thing. I'll still be here."

I picture him sitting there all night. Waiting for my answer. And only one answer will do.

SARAH

I hear him before I see him, the twigs snapping under his boots.

"What did they want?"

There's a knot of fear in the pit of my stomach.

"They want me to help them, help the government."

"Why you?"

"Because of my . . . gift. I can see where trouble's coming and get people away from it. Like I did in the Chaos."

"Adam, these are the same people that tried to stop you then. What's changed?"

"I think they just understand now that I can be useful. They see me as a leader."

This sounds like bullshit to me.

"I don't trust them," I say.

"Neither do I," he says, "but they're saying we can go with them, go to somewhere warm and dry, where they've got doctors, electricity, everything we haven't had for two years. You want to settle somewhere, Sarah. You want somewhere safe for Marty and Luke, and Mia and the baby. This could be it."

"I thought we'd found it here."

"Here's still living in a tent in the woods, isn't it? What Saul's talking about is different. Back to civilization. You can tell they've all had enough food. They're well kitted out. They've come from somewhere that's OK."

Somewhere that's OK. In my head I'm back at my parents' house, before the quake, before I ran away. There's deep soft carpet under my bare toes, I'm sinking into a claw-foot bath full of bubbles, watching Hollywood blockbusters on a wall-sized screen. I've got everything . . . the sort of life people dream about. But it's rotten to the core.

My family was poisoned and the house was a beautiful cage in which my dad could do whatever He wanted. And He did—night after night after night.

"People make a home, Adam. You said that. And that man's a thug. You saw what he did to Mia."

"But we can save Mia and your brothers from living like animals. Think about it. Regular food, a roof over our heads."

"I don't know. I don't trust him."

"You haven't heard what he's offering. You talk to him in the morning. You'll see."

I look at him closely. There's something about him. His eyes are flicking all over the place.

He's not being straight with me.

At first light, we leave the boys and Mia sleeping, and make our way to where I left Saul. He's still sitting next to the fire, waiting, just the way he said he would. The other two aren't there. The sleeping bags and the rifles have gone.

Sarah fires questions at him. She's like a Rottweiler, more like she used to be when we first got together. I love that feistiness. It gets butterflies going in my stomach. But I can tell Saul's impatient.

He don't want to answer her, don't want to tell us exactly where we'd be going. All we get is "south" and then, eventually, "the Cotswolds." I don't even know what the Cotswolds is, or are.

"That must be fifty miles from here," Sarah says. She obviously knows more than me. "How would we get there?"

"Got some big bikes here. Take an hour or so, that's all."

"There are five of us and three of you. Anyway, Mia can't go on a bike and I don't think the boys should, either, and I can't —"

She stops midsentence and I realize she doesn't want Saul to know about the baby. But she's pulling her coat farther around her and instead of hiding her stomach, it just draws attention to it.

Saul looks her up and down, and I know the penny's dropped.

"You're right, Sarah," he says. "Eight into three doesn't go. So it's one rider, one pillion per bike. Up to three passengers—Adam, you, and Mia, if you like."

Just for a moment her jaw drops. "No," she says. "Never. We won't leave my brothers. Adam, tell him. Tell him!"

"This isn't a time for selfishness—it's a time to think about what we can do for others," Saul says smoothly.

"Are you saying I'm selfish to care about my family?" She's really riled now.

"No, but there's a bigger picture here. I know Adam is important to you but he's also important to all of us."

They both turn to look at me.

I'm thinking warm beds. I'm thinking hot food. I'm thinking helping people, using the numbers like I did before. But I know Sarah's right. I have to be with her now, I *want* to be with her, and she ain't going nowhere without the boys.

"Not now, Saul," I say. "We'll stay here for the winter."

I put my hands on Sarah's shoulders, and feel the tension go out of them. It gives me the thrill I always get when I touch her and she responds. This connection we have doesn't always need words.

"Is that it?" he says. "Your final word?" There's a warning note in his voice, but it don't matter what he says now. I've made my mind up and I know it's the right thing to do.

"Yeah," I say firmly. "That's it."

He clenches his jaw and there's a flash of temper in his eyes. He looks around quickly, like he's scoping out who's where. Then he turns back to me.

"In that case you don't give me any option." He lunges toward me, grabs my wrist, shoves me around, and twists my arm up behind my back. "I'm arresting you, Adam Dawson. You've got a murder charge to answer, or had you forgotten?"

Sarah's barged out of the way and she staggers sideways. It's all so quick, I don't have time to react. He's yanking my arm up so hard it feels like it's going to come out of its socket.

"Bastard!" I gasp. He pulls harder.

"Let him go."

I look up and I'm staring at the barrel of a gun, but it's not aimed at me.

Daniel's got Saul in his sights.

"Let him go," he says again. He's calm, his eyes fixed on Saul.

"I'm acting for the government," Saul spits. "You can't pull a gun on me."

"I don't give a stuff about *your* government. This is my camp. You're not welcome here anymore. Let Adam go and get out."

For a few seconds there's silence. Daniel and Saul stare each other down. I can't tell who's going to crack. All I can hear is the blood pounding in my ears as Saul tightens his grip on my wrist. Then he drops it. My arm flops to my side. I stumble a couple of paces away from Saul, then turn and face him. I want to slam my fist in his face.

"That's it, Adam. Step away from him." Daniel's in control. For such a chill guy, he does a good job as a Wild West sheriff. "Right. Now you, Saul, get out of here, and don't come back. If I see your face in our camp again, it'll get blown off."

Saul backs away with his hands up. His face is like thunder.

Watching him, I feel cold inside. He's not the sort of bloke who forgives and forgets.

Fifty feet away, he turns and stalks off into the forest. A moment later we hear the motorcycles starting up.

I turn to Daniel. "Thanks, man," I say.

"No problem. You're a legend, Adam. That guy, Saul, I'm guessing he's trying to neutralize you."

"What?"

"Take you out of circulation, away from the people who need you."

"Who needs me?"

Daniel looks surprised. "All of us. He was right about that — you're important to all of us. And you'll always have friends here. Always."

I look him in the eye. 05312066. There's no always, not for anyone, but I get what he's trying to say and I appreciate it.

"Cheers," I say, and I go to high-five him, but he grabs my hand and pulls me in for a hug. A bit of backslapping and we draw apart. I'm blinking hard, trying to keep the tears away. Sarah was right to remind me. It's people that matter.

"What do you think they'll do next?" Daniel asks.

"I dunno. Don't think they'll leave it at that. We should move on, I s'pose, get out of your hair."

"No, Adam," he says, "stay here. You're welcome. We've all been hoping you'd come."

"Sarah?"

She's quiet and pale beside me, almost ghostlike.

"I don't like guns," she says.

I put my arm around her. "They've gone now. It's alright."

"They've gone now. But they'll be back."

Arm in arm, we walk through the camp to our tent. After the tension of the last twelve hours, it feels like the whole place is breathing a sigh of relief. People are tending to their fires, listening to the sound of the motorbikes leaving. There was a frost last night and now the sunlight filters through the branches above us, making the ground sparkle.

Then I hear Marty and Luke. They're yelling.

Sarah and I break apart from each other and run.

First I see Luke lying outside the tent, clutching his face.

Then Marty running toward us, his face streaked with tears.

Finally, I see the back of the tent. It's slashed from top to bottom.

"Mia . . . Mia . . ." is all Marty can say. His breath's coming in ragged bursts.

I sprint toward the tent and dive in.

Mia's bed is empty.

She's gone.

SARAH

They've taken her.

For a moment I'm paralyzed. I'm looking past Adam at that gaping hole, the edge of the tent flapping gently.

We've only been gone a few minutes. Someone must have been watching, waiting. Saul's men. While we were talking to him . . .

"Marty, tell me. What did you see?" I grip his shoulders. He tries to squirm away from me, still crying. I shake him. "What did you see?" I scream.

"It was those men," he sobs. "One hit Luke in the face. The other took Mia. . . . Don't shout. It's not my fault. It . . ."

Adam's on his feet and running into the forest.

"I'm sorry. I'm sorry, Marty," I say. "I didn't mean to . . . Stay there, and look after Luke. I'll be back."

And then I'm running, too, as best I can, thrashing through frosty brushwood, crunching, slipping, scrambling after Adam. He's heading toward the road. I can hear the engines revving and stuttering. They're not clear of the woods yet. Maybe it's not too late.

I'm way behind Adam. He's fast. I used to be, but now the baby throws me off balance and slows me down. I clasp my hands around my stomach to try to protect the little one as I lurch forward. There's pure adrenaline in my veins now. I have to reach Mia. I *have* to. I reach the road a split second before the riders do. They skid around and face us: one, two, three.

Mia's on the second motorcycle. She's wrapped in her striped blanket and the big man with the long hair is holding her, his beefy arm clamped around her middle. She's struggling. My heart skips a beat.

"Mia!" I scream, and for a moment she stops struggling

and looks up. Her face is a picture of terror. "Mia!"

Adam's sprinting toward the motorbikes, trying to block their path. It's insane. The machines are huge — great hunks of angry metal. Saul and his thugs aren't fazed by us. They pause for a second, no more, then they rev up and launch themselves forward, in our direction.

I don't want Mia's motorcycle to crash, but I can't just let them go without trying to stop them. Saul blasts past first. Adam jumps out of the way. His eyes are on Mia and the second motorcycle. He tries to grab the handlebars. The bike swerves away from him and toward me. The wing-view mirror hits me in the chest, and I'm thrown backward. The third bike weaves to the left and then they're away, accelerating down the road.

"No! No! Mia!"

There's an explosion next to me. Then another and another.

It's Daniel. He's shooting right at them. One of the motor-cycles skids and goes over, sliding along the road. Something's thrown clear.

"Stop it! Stop it!" I heave myself up, teeth gritted against the pain, and throw myself at him, putting both hands on the barrel of his gun and pushing it up toward the sky.

"I'm going for their tires!"

"Mia's on one of them. Stop it!"

He drops the gun away from his face. The other two bikes are slowing — they've twigged that they're a man down. From here, I can't work out who's on the ground. Was it the second motorcycle that went down? Is it Mia? Adam and Daniel and I start running at the same time. I'm in agony, but I don't stop.

One of the bikes is turning around; the other is continuing on down the road. I stretch my legs out, cradle my stomach with my hands, willing myself to go faster. All I can think of is Mia.

The motorcycle's going to get there first.

I'm minutes away now as it screams to a halt. Adam's closer. The rider dismounts. It's Saul.

I'm shouting as I'm running now, "Mia! Mia! Mia!" But he can't hear me or he doesn't care. He's crouching down, examining the body on the ground. A pool of dark liquid is spreading out over the tarmac.

One body. It's the wiry man.

Mia's on the other motorcycle with the long-haired man. She's gone.

"Saul! Saul! Please . . ." I'm gasping now, gasping and sobbing, stumbling toward him.

No reaction. He doesn't turn his head. He doesn't look my way — or at Adam, or Daniel. Instead, he gets to his feet, pulls a revolver from his belt, holds his arm out straight, the barrel pointing at the man's chest, and shoots three times.

The body jerks with the force of the bullets. We stop in our tracks, appalled, terrified.

It's only then that Saul seems to notice Adam and Daniel and me. He looks up and swings his straightened arm toward us. All my breath seems to leave my body.

"Drop your gun, put your hands up, and keep them up."

Daniel drops his rifle and we do as we're told. Saul's eyes are cold and steely.

He points the revolver at Daniel.

"You shot at me, and you shot at my men," he says. He is completely calm.

He fires.

Daniel falls to the ground, screaming and clutching his knee.

I'm screaming, too. The barrel of the gun moves in my direction.

"Shut up, Sarah."

It could be my turn next. My legs are shaking now.

"Adam, pick this bike up," Saul barks.

"What?" Adam's in shock. His eyes are almost blank with terror.

"Pick this bike up. Now. Do it."

Still with his hands above his head, Adam stumbles to the bike. The engine's still running. He hesitates.

"Stand it up."

He tries to wrestle the motorcycle upright. It's a beast of a machine and it takes him a couple of goes to manage it. Saul looks at him with barely disguised contempt.

"Can you ride one of these?"

"I've never tried."

"Put it on its stand. You kick it out. Now take his helmet."

"What?"

"You heard me."

Adam stares at the corpse on the ground and the black pool of blood around it.

"I don't wannit."

"It's not for you. It's for Sarah."

The sound of my name makes my blood freeze. I'm going, too. My stomach contracts, the skin as tight as a drum across the baby inside me.

"No," I croak. "Not on a motorbike." I don't want to say it, but I have to. "I'm pregnant, Saul. Don't make me ride a motorcycle."

"You'll sit behind me." He's immovable. Inhuman.

"I don't want to. You can't make me."

He points his gun directly at me.

"Can't I? Shut up and get that helmet on."

Adam's crouching down by the wiry man's side. He supports his lifeless head and undoes the buckle with shaking hands. The helmet gets stuck when he tries to lift it off and he yanks at it. It comes loose but the man's head thumps down onto the surface of the road.

"God. Oh God," Adam says.

"Don't worry," says Saul. "He didn't feel a thing. Give the helmet to Sarah and then get on that bike."

The thought of putting on a dead man's helmet, his blood going in my hair, is making me gag.

"We just have to do it," Adam says to me under his breath. "It'll be safer for you. Be brave." He raises the helmet over my head and brings it down.

Saul mounts his bike and pats the saddle behind him with the gun.

"The boys? What about my brothers?" I say. My voice is muffled by the helmet.

"Get on, Sarah," says Saul, bringing his gun up once more. "I'm not going to ask you again."

Adam helps me onto Saul's bike. I take one last look at Daniel. His eyes are closing, the blood from his leg pouring onto the road.

Marty, Luke . . . It's too quick. There's no time to tell them anything. I can only hope they'll be looked after. Someone, surely someone, will look after them.

"Put your hands on my waist," Saul says.

What choice do I have? I reach forward and grip the leather of his coat. Touching him makes me feel sick.

Adam clambers onto the other bike.

"Come on," Saul shouts, "we've got some catching up to do! Let's go. Kick it into first gear with your left foot. Throttle's on the right handlebar, twist it to go faster. Brake lever's there, too. Clutch is on the left. You'll get it."

He sits, watching as Adam's hands fumble at the controls.

"Kick it with your left foot and twist the throttle," Saul repeats.

Adam's bike jerks forward and he nearly topples off. He pulls up, then tries again. This time it's smoother. I watch over Saul's shoulder as he starts to weave down the road.

Then Saul starts his engine up and I get the fright of

my life. It's like the thing's alive—the noise, the smell, the vibration is overwhelming. I grip Saul tighter. I have to.

Suddenly, we're lurching forward and my butt's sliding back. I dig my fingertips into Saul's body as the world around us becomes a blur.

Who is the man I'm holding on to for dear life? This cold-blooded murderer? And what does he want with us?

ADAM

I've never ridden anything bigger than a scooter before and this is a massive, supercharged machine. Saul and his mate look like they belong on these things with their leathers and their gloves and their Nazi-style helmets. I got nothing. I'm driving this thing in a hoodie and jeans, like a kid on a carnival ride, only this is more frightening than any theme park.

I'm so scared I can hardly breathe. If I wipe out I'll be raspberry jam all over the road. There are potholes and cracks all over the place. I do my best to steer a good course, but in my mind I keep seeing that guy lying in the pool of blood.

Don't think about it. Concentrate.

I run through the controls in my head—right for brake and throttle, left for clutch. The clutch has got me boggled: As I increase the throttle, the engine's roar goes up and up, like a wasp singing scales. I try to change gear, but I don't get it. The engine jerks and kicks, but it don't change up. The bike's screaming now, and it's rattling my brain against the inside of my skull. I have another go and the clutch bites this time, the roar dampens down.

I can do this. I can do it.

I can hear Saul behind me now, but I can't see the other bike ahead yet. Is Mia OK? She was kicking and struggling before—I hope to God she's staying still. Still and safe. I have to get to her. Whatever weird power she might have, she's still just a little girl. Sarah's little girl and the one who calls me Daddy.

I twist the throttle again and the bike surges forward.

After two years of walking, traveling at this speed is a buzz. If I wasn't so shit-scared for Mia and Sarah, I might even enjoy it. The world looks different from the saddle of a motorcycle. You lose the detail, the edges are blurred, but your senses sharpen up. There's the wind on your face, the smell of oil in your nostrils, the pulsing of the engine in your hands and legs.

One more twist on the throttle and at last I get a glimpse of the back of a bike ahead. *Yes, I'm catching them.*

The noise from Saul's bike is getting louder. I twist around to see how close he is and the bike tips under me, veering across the road. Shit! I lean the other way and it rights itself, threatening to tip over the other way. I wrestle with it 'til I can feel the balance again.

Saul is only ten feet or so behind.

And now I'm back to thinking about him firing his revolver into the guy on the ground. *Bang, bang, bang.* Just like that. I seen things before, bad things, especially during the Chaos when it felt like all the normal rules had gone and people were just looking out for themselves. I seen fights. I seen people pulling knives on each other. But I never seen something that cold-blooded. It was like he was putting down an animal. And then he turned his gun on Daniel. . . .

But Dan's number is sometime in 2066. He should be OK, if it don't change. If, if, if . . .

Now I'm thinking about Saul's number, too, the way it shimmers in and out of focus. Just like Mia's.

Just like Mia's. Just like Mia's.

It goes around and around in my head.

Saul's bike draws level. Sarah's leaning forward, holding him around the waist. Her face is white as a sheet, she's gritting her teeth so hard her jawbone's almost jutting through her skin. I don't know how much more of this she can take. I feel a stab of guilt in my guts. I'm meant to be protecting her, her and the baby. And now look at her. She's terrified. Saul lifts one hand off the handlebars and gives me a mock salute. Our eyes meet and I get a flash of his shimmering number.

Just like Mia's.

I tear my eyes away, but it's too late.

There's a crack in the tarmac across my side of the road and my front wheel hits it square on, then skews around. The handlebars are wrenched sideways out of my hands and suddenly I'm flying, my feet flung up above my head—and the last thing I hear is the sound of Sarah screaming.

SARAH

From the start Adam never looked in control of the motorcycle. Over Saul's shoulder I watched him struggling with it, fighting to keep his balance. He was an accident waiting to happen.

And now it has.

His body is powerless against the laws of physics. Velocity, resistance, momentum.

He lands some fifteen feet away from his bike, smack down on his back, hands and feet hitting the ground a split second later. There are motorcycle bits raining down around him. And then nothing. No movement, no noise, apart from our engine and my screams.

I slam into Saul's back as he brakes.

"Get off," he says, but I'm on the ground and cradling Adam's face before Saul's even got the motorcycle on its stand.

"Adam! Adam, can you hear me?"

His eyes are closed. He's out cold.

"Let me," Saul says. "Move!" He pushes me roughly to one side and puts his fingers to Adam's neck. "There's a pulse." He moves his hand in front of Adam's nose. "And he's breathing."

He sounds so relieved it's almost odd.

He reaches into the inside of his jacket and brings out a phone. I haven't seen one for two years.

"Man down!" he shouts. "We're on the A46, north of the M4 junction. Launch a drone and get a fix on me. I need an ambulance here ASAP."

He ends the call and turns his attention back to Adam.

"The medics will be here in twenty minutes," he says, almost to himself. It's as if I'm not there. "They'll assess his neck and back. His brain function."

Neck, back, brain function. Oh God, this is bad. Really, really bad.

Twenty minutes.

Each second is like an hour.

I scan Adam's face, his fingers, his feet, looking for the slightest movement, the smallest sign. But there's nothing. He just looks like he's asleep, except that I know he's normally restless in his sleep, as restless as he is awake; his legs twitch, he mutters and mumbles, he turns onto one side and then the other.

Now he's perfectly still.

Saul paces back and forth, peering down the road, but I can't leave Adam's side.

You never know what you've got until you lose it. And now I know I don't want to lose him. I desperately, desperately don't want to lose him. How could I ever have doubted it?

The ambulance—a four-wheel drive—doesn't announce itself with a siren. There's no need. Since the Chaos, there've been no cars on the road. Four people jump out. They fire questions at Saul—what, when, how?—and all the time they're getting to work on Adam.

"Is he . . . ?" I splutter. "Will he . . . ?" No one hears me. I'm pushed outside their circle and all I can do is peer through the gaps.

They fix a neck brace onto him, then ease him onto a stretcher.

"Can I go with him in the ambulance? Please?"

Again, I'm ignored.

"Get back on the bike," Saul says curtly. It's the first time he's spoken to me since the accident. "We'll get there before they do."

The bike. I can't face it. My legs ache and my chest hurts where the mirror of the other bike hit it. The skin across my stomach is stretched and sore.

"Please," I say.

He barely looks at me. "You can get on the bike or I can leave you here. Doesn't make any difference to me. I only brought you along so Adam would come. You might still be useful to us, but I doubt it."

In that moment, I understand I mean nothing to this man. Literally, nothing. He'd leave me at the side of the road, in the middle of nowhere, without a second thought. With my boyfriend in an ambulance, my daughter kidnapped, and a baby on the way. This poor baby; starved and lumped about and now battered and bruised.

I feel numb, helpless, like all I can do is watch while the world spins out of control around me.

I get on the bike.

· · ·

We set off before the ambulance does, crossing a bridge over a motorway. Three years ago there would have been bumper-to-bumper traffic. Today, there's a string of tents along the hard shoulder on one side and two people on horseback on the other. The road runs between gently rolling fields. We pass signs for Chippenham, Corsham, and Bath, and I wonder if we're heading for one of them when Saul starts braking.

I'm confused. There's nothing there, just a track leading to a dull-looking hill. I'm expecting the track to go up, or around. But it doesn't. It carries straight on. And then I see it: a large metal door set into the hillside. A pair of uniformed men, armed with the same rifles as Saul and his men, stand on either side.

A bunker.

We come to a stop by the metal door. The armed men salute, and one of them slides back a bolt before pulling the door open.

I don't want to be buried in there, shut in with no light, no fresh air. I can't do it.

"Is Mia here?" I say to Saul's back.

He doesn't bother answering me, just kills the engine and dismounts.

"Get off the bike," he says.

I don't move. I don't want to go inside the hill.

"I'm losing patience, Sarah," Saul murmurs, then, before I can say anything, he grabs me around my waist with one arm and hauls me off the bike. I stagger as my feet hit the ground. My joints are in agony.

"Can you give me a minute?" I ask. "I just need to stretch my legs —"

"Stretch them inside," he snaps.

I look at the entrance in front of us — a square of light in the hillside, a bright, empty corridor maybe fifty feet long — and then I really start to panic. My breath is tight in my throat, I've got goose bumps everywhere, and my scalp's tingling.

If I go in, I'll never come out.

"Is Mia inside?" I ask again.

Saul pauses for a moment, as if debating whether the information might be useful — to him.

"She's here," he says eventually.

Is he telling me the truth? I have no way of knowing.

But there's only one way to find out.

The corridor is empty apart from a few wooden chairs lining the walls. The artificial glare of fluorescent lights on the ceiling hurts my eyes. At the end of the corridor is a metal grid, and behind that is something that looks like an elevator door.

I follow Saul to the grid. He presses a button on the wall, but there's already a whirring and whining sound. The lift thunks to a halt. Then the door concertinas open to reveal a squad of people in white coats, and another uniformed guard. He slides open the metal grid.

The white-coats barge past us on the double, heading to the bunker entrance.

"Adam Dawson's ETA five minutes," Saul says to one as he passes.

The man merely nods. He's wearing a tweed jacket under his white coat. None of the other white-coats looks at me. It's as if I've become invisible.

I step into the lift. It's huge, easily big enough for twenty people. It's an antique, though—the control panel isn't a set of buttons but a retro dial with a metal handle. I hear the grid slide shut behind me, and I spin around.

Saul's standing on the other side of the grid. "This is Sarah," he says to the guard. "I'm going to wait for Adam. He's the important one." His piercing black eyes turn on me. There's a mocking glint in them. "Don't worry, Sarah. It's sixty feet deep, you know. Safest place in England. Just one way in, and one way out."

"I want to see Mia," I say. "And Adam."

"You will," he replies, turning his back on me.

I'm dismissed. Unimportant.

The guard heaves the lift door shut, then winds the handle to DOWN.

The whole thing judders. Instinctively I clutch at my stomach as the lift starts to drop into the earth.

"It's all right," I say under my breath, but I don't know who I'm trying to convince—the baby or myself. Either way, the words are feeble and empty.

We plunge downward into the unknown.

What the hell is this place?

ADAM

I can hear voices.

"We've got eye movement. . . . He's coming around. . . ."

Who are they talking about?

"Adam. Adam, can you hear me?"

Now they're shouting at someone called Adam. I feel sorry for the poor sod, whoever he is, with people yelling at him like that.

I open my eyes a little but the light's so bright I shut them again quickly.

"Did you see that? He's back. Adam! Adam!"

I open my eyes again, and a circle of faces begins to drift into focus. Am I meant to know these people? I look from one to the other. They're faces with eyes and noses and mouths and numbers, but I've no idea who they are or who I am or where I am. All I know is I'm alive and breathing. *What happened?*

One of them's talking to me now. Face like it's been

squashed in a lift door. 11082034. Fifty-something, tweed jacket under a white coat. His hair's too brown, not a hint of gray, parted on one side and hanging in two curtains on either side of his puffy cheeks.

"Adam, if you can understand me, blink now."

I understand him, I'm just not sure I'm called Adam, but I blink anyway. A ripple of excitement runs around the circle of faces.

"Good," he says. "Now can you squeeze my hand?"

I peer down my body, past the big collar thing around my neck. The guy's holding my left hand now. Bloody hell, I don't even know him, do I? His chubby fingers squeeze mine.

"Can you feel that? Can you squeeze back?"

I squeeze back.

"Excellent."

He works his way around my body. Arms, hands, legs, and feet—all in working order.

"Remarkable," he says. I don't know him, but I'm pleased he's pleased. I start to relax. "What's my number, Adam?"

He asks it all casual, just lobs it in like any of his other questions, but it's not the same. I don't feel relaxed now. Alarm bells are going off in my head. Then I hear another voice. But it's not someone in this room. The voice is in my head.

"You mustn't tell, Adam. Not anyone. Not ever."

"I dunno," I say.

Tweed Jacket looms over me. "You don't know? Are you sure? What's my number, Adam?"

"That's enough. Leave it, Newsome. Let's get him downstairs. He should sleep." It's another voice speaking, deep and sharp. I move my eyes. There's a man standing on the other side of me. He's got cropped gray hair and a scar above his left eye. His number's shimmering as I try to get a fix on it. I've seen him before. My mind's racing to remember, trying to place him, but I can't get there.

Tweed Jacket straightens up.

"Of course," he says. "We'll try again tomorrow."

The crowd thins out.

I close my eyes again, but I'm not sleepy. I'm going over and over what I've just seen, what I know. The faces, the numbers . . . and that voice.

"You mustn't tell."

She called me Adam, too, the woman in my head, so it must be true.

I'm Adam.

Adam who?

SARAH

The lift thunks down. We're at the bottom. The guard winds the handle to OPEN and then drags the door back to reveal another corridor. This one's dimly lit and concrete and so long

I can't see where it ends. The walls are lined with gurgling pipes and punctuated by metal doors with shuttered grilles at eye level, keyholes, and numbers. Everything's painted battleship gray. It's like a prison.

The guard takes my arm. I try to shrug him off, but his hold is firm. Am I a prisoner? I look at him properly for the first time.

He's young, not much older than me. He's got the beginnings of a mustache, and his military beret doesn't seem to sit at the regulation angle. He glances at me nervously.

"I'm to take you to see your daughter," he says. "We're trying to . . . settle her in."

Mia. She's here. Relief floods through me. And now I don't care about Saul and the soldiers and how weird this place is. I just want to see Mia.

The squaddie leads the way, deeper and deeper into the tunnel. He mutters something about food and a bed, but I don't really take it in. Our footsteps echo dully on the concrete floor. I can hear a low mechanical throbbing in the background.

Every step feels like a step away from life and light and everything else I've ever known, but it's also a step closer to Mia and that's what matters. I try to note where we're going, but we turn so many corners, pass so many doors, and everything looks the same battleship gray, I soon give up.

Then I hear a sound that makes me freeze. A child crying. The noise is faint but unmistakable. Mia.

We stop next to what looks like a prison door. It has a

number: 1214. The guard taps on it, and it swings open. Mia's voice blasts out into the corridor. I get a glimpse of a square, plain room, a single bed in the corner. A woman is sitting on the bed and next to her is Mia, her face twisted up and beetroot red, her arms and legs flailing.

"Mia!" I shout. "Mia!" I push past the guard and rush into the room. He doesn't stop me.

Mia stops midscream and opens her eyes, then she throws herself at me, clinging to me like a little monkey, sobbing. I kiss her hair, hug her to me.

The woman stands up. "She was starting to settle," she says unconvincingly.

At the sound of her voice, Mia increases the volume of her yells.

That's my girl, Mia, I think. *Give her hell.*

The woman looks offended as she sweeps from the room, slamming the door behind her. I hear a key turn in the lock. There are towels on the bed and clothes in two sizes. But the walls are bare and there's no window. It's a cell.

"We're locked in, Mia," I say, trying to control my sudden panic.

She lifts her head up from my shoulder. Her eyes are puffy from crying, her breath is hot in my face. We might be prisoners, but Mia's here. She's alive.

"Locked in," she repeats.

I hug her closer and look around the room. There's a bathroom connected to it—for a moment, I think of running water, having a hot shower for the first time in two years.

"Let's have a wash," I say.

The bathroom's basic but clean. I turn on the shower. The pipes creak and groan, then hot water squirts out of the showerhead.

Mia shakes her head, clings to me harder.

"Mia, it's like rain — nice, warm rain. You'll like it."

I'm not taking no for an answer. I undress myself, then Mia, ignoring her protests. Holding her hand, I step into the shower, pulling her in gently after me. I tip shampoo into the palm of my hand and rub it into our scalps. The shampoo, the soap, the steam, and the water all smell clinical, like we're in a hospital. But they're doing their job. The water draining away around our feet is gray. Bits of twig and leaf stick in the plughole.

We step out of the shower and I wrap a towel around me while I get Mia dry and dressed. Soon she's all pink and clean and warm. The smaller clothes on the bed are too big but she snuggles into them anyway.

When I hold up the others, it's obvious they weren't expecting me to be pregnant. There are underclothes and a T-shirt, sweatshirt, and track pants. The bottoms are stretchy but they're still pretty tight over my stomach. We sit on the bed. I've got one arm round Mia and the other cradling the baby inside me.

I take in the chemical smell of the shower lingering in

the room, stare at the lock in the metal door and at the blank, windowless walls.

Where is the air coming from? How can we breathe in here, sixty feet down?

"Safest place in England. Just one way in, and one way out."

I don't care what that man said. We can't stay here. I've got to get us out, all of us.

ADAM

I go in and out of sleep for hours. I don't know how long, but there's always some stranger there when I wake up, and there are always questions.

"How are you?"

"Can you feel this?"

"How many fingers am I holding up?"

And there are tests—temperature, blood pressure, pupil reaction to light.

And sometimes there are injections. They soften the edges of the room, the people around me—the nurses, the guy with the tweed jacket, the guy with the scar and the shimmering number—and the mattress I'm lying on. They blur the thoughts in my head and before I know it, I'm asleep again.

This time when I wake up I don't want to go back to sleep. Somewhere between dreaming and waking I've remembered who that voice was.

My mum. ·

I can see her now. I can see it all.

She was only little, but, boy, was she tough. No Dad, just Mum. We lived by the seaside. We'd walk on the sand, walk for miles and miles. I'd chase the seagulls. There were ice-cream cones, donkey rides.

Jem Marsh. That's who she was.

And I'm her son. Adam.

I'm Adam.

And that's where the numbers came from. She saw them, too, when she was growing up. She understood and she tried to help me, even after she died. I feel a stab of grief just under my ribs as I realize she's dead. It's like losing her for the first time. I've only just remembered her and now she's died again. My mum's dead.

Those words I heard, about not telling, she never said them to me. She wrote them in a letter I only got after she died. I remember every word on that paper, and I remember who gave it to me.

Nan.

I can see her, too. Perched at the kitchen counter in her grotty house in West London. Her hair a brilliant, ridiculous purple. "My crowning glory," she'd say. She scared the shit out of me at first—I thought she was my worst nightmare. But I loved her. The inside of my nose tingles as I inhale the smoke from her cigarette. "I'll be the last smoker in England," she said once, stubborn-minded and proud of it. . . .

The smoke takes me somewhere else. . . .

I'm sitting by a bonfire, in the middle of the woods. I'm in a circle, a circle of friends, and I've got my arms around a girl. She must be my girl if I'm holding her like that. She's got her back to me and I've got my arms around her waist, my chin's resting on the top of her head. I kiss her hair and she twists her face up toward mine, and I see her blue, blue eyes. My God, I could get lost in those eyes. Her number's a beautiful thing, not full of sadness and horror like most of them. I get a comforting feeling from it, like it's washed through with love.

This girl. My girl. What's her name? Is she still mine? Where is she?

"Time for another shot."

They're back again. Two people in white coats.

No! Not now. Not yet.

I try to fight them off, but I'm outnumbered. There's two of them for a reason; one to hold you down, the other to stick in the needle.

"Have you got him?"

"Yes. Quick, though."

I don't want it. I want to stay awake, to hold on to my memories. . . . Mum, Nan, my girl . . .

Where I am? What is happening to me?

I can't see her. I've lost her. She's gone.

I've lost Mia in this cold and lonely place. I scream her name, over and over, until my throat is hoarse. My voice is swallowed by the fog, absorbed by the trees and the stones.

"Mia! Mia!"

How could I let her out of my sight? I only looked away for a second and she was gone. The gravel crunches under my feet and I leave the path and walk through and around and over the graves until the pain stops me again and I have to stand, gripping on to a stone, closing my eyes, trying to breathe.

When I open my eyes again, she'll be here. She'll smile at me and hold her arms up for a cuddle.

I open my eyes. She's not there.

• • •

"Mummy! Mum-meee!"

Mia's shaking my shoulder.

"What? What is it?"

"Mummy shouting."

"Was I? Did I wake you up?"

This place is pitch-black. I don't know where we are or whether it's night or day. I can't smell the musty closeness of our tent, and there's no breeze. The air is perfectly still. But Mia is here. And right now that seems terribly, terribly important. I can't remember the dream anymore, but hearing her voice, feeling her little hands digging into my shoulder feels like the answer to a prayer.

I put my arms around her and she snuggles in close. My eyes start to make some sense of the darkness. There's a strip of light at the top and bottom of a door, and a bright rectangle where a grille's half open. And now I remember.

We're in a room, a cell.

Mia and me.

But Adam . . . Where's Adam? There was a crash. He was flying through the air. Saul said they were bringing him here, but did he arrive? Is he OK? Is he still alive?

I've got Mia snuggled close, but suddenly, this cell seems like a lonely place. It doesn't feel right without Adam.

"Let's go back to sleep, Mia," I say, although I know I won't be sleeping anytime soon. "Shall we sing 'Twinkle'?"

I start singing. But Mia doesn't join in. Halfway through, she reaches up and puts her hand on my mouth. It stops me in my tracks. "No stars," she says.

"You don't want 'Twinkle'?"

"No stars," she says again, and she points to the ceiling. And then I get it, how strange it must be for Mia to sleep indoors.

"Oh," I say. "We can't see the stars here, Mia, but they're still out there. They haven't gone away. They're waiting for us. They can hear us when we sing."

I start again, and this time Mia joins in. We sing together

until her voice trails off and her breathing becomes regular and heavy.

She's asleep. I hope she's somewhere different, somewhere better than this place. I wish I could sleep, too, but I can't. Inside me, the baby shifts restlessly. Will he or she learn to love the stars, too?

I can hear someone shouting, a long way away. A man's voice, screaming in the night. Then footsteps, quiet at first, but getting louder, until they're outside my door. They stop. My heart skips a beat. There are voices, low, male.

I'm trying to think what I could use as a weapon if they come in. There's nothing.

I can make out the odd word, but I can't make sense of their conversation. It ends with a joke, though. Two deep voices laughing in chorus. Are they laughing at me, at us?

Then footsteps start up again, getting fainter until they're finally gone. But this time it's only one set of steps, and there were two voices. Is someone still there?

Mia's arm is slung across my body. I lift it up carefully and lay it on top of her, then I ease out from under the covers and tiptoe across the room.

I look through the peephole. My stomach turns over.

There's an eye looking in, only a few inches away from mine.

"Who are you?" I whisper. I'm scared of getting an answer, scared of not getting one. I'm back in the house where I grew up. *There's a door and a man outside and I'm trapped.*

My dad's dead but the panic's still there, waiting to get me. Waiting for moments like this. I hold my breath.

The eye blinks, once, twice, and moves away.

ADAM

"You're doing very well, Adam. Your cognitive functions are excellent, considering what you went through yesterday."

It's the guy with the squished face again. Newsome. He's asking the questions now, doing more checks. And next to him, sitting silently, is Gray-hair, the guy with the scar and the shimmering number. Every time I look at him, the violence of his number hits me. It's sickening and mesmerizing at the same time. There's something about that number . . . but I can't get it. Not right now.

"Excellent," Newsome says. "So now it's time for some more sophisticated tests."

Before I know what's happening, the assistant has put a leather strap through the arm of my chair and buckled it around my right wrist.

"What the —?"

"Just a precaution."

"No, no, I don't want this."

"We can't have movement or the tests won't work."

I try to fight back, but I'm weak and there are two of them now. My left wrist is held down and strapped, too.

Another assistant wheels forward a trolley with monitors and a bunch of wires like spaghetti on it. As he looms nearer I realize he's gonna attach most of these wires to my head.

"No —"

"It's all part of the assessment of your condition," Newsome says smoothly. "Essential medical treatment. Nothing more. Just sit back. Try to relax."

I can't do anything *but* sit there, but my jaw's clenched and my arms and legs are tense and stiff as they tape me up. They don't need to shave my head: Most of my hair was burned off when I fell in the fire the night Junior died, and the rest is so short they've got no trouble attaching the electrodes.

They wire up my chest, too, so they can monitor my heart through the tests. And my fingertips. What's that all about? Looks like something out of a spy film. Isn't that what they do to see if you're lying?

"No way. Stop it. Stop!"

This feels wrong. Really wrong.

Newsome has set up two other chairs facing me, about three feet away. Now he sits in one and Gray-hair sits in the other. He still hasn't said a word. But his eyes . . . those dark eyes . . . and that number. . . . I can't tear my own eyes away.

"I'm going to ask you some questions," Newsome says, "and I want you to fire the answers back at me. First thing that comes into your head."

"OK." I feel my temper flare. "Undo the straps."

"What?"

"That's what's in my head right now."

"I haven't started yet. I haven't asked you a question."

He's getting irritated. But he started this with the wrist-straps. I'm not going to make it easy for him.

He turns to the bank of monitors next to him and fiddles with a couple of controls. He keeps reaching up, tucking his hair behind his ear—the thick, brown hair that looks twenty years younger than him. It's a wig. It's got to be a wig.

"What are you thinking?" he says. I hesitate, and he leaps in. "What's in there right now? Right now." He snaps a finger in front of my face.

"I was wondering . . . who cut your hair."

One of the assistants stifles a laugh. I think I see the corner of Gray-hair's mouth twitch, but I'm not sure. Newsome's eyes narrow, just a little bit, and some color creeps into his face. He turns away and makes like he's checking the monitors, then turns back to me.

"What's your name?"

Start with the easy ones.

"Adam."

"Adam who?"

"Adam . . . Marsh." My mum was a Marsh. Am I, too? I can't remember.

"How old are you?"

"Seventeen."

"What's your date of birth?"

"Twenty-second of August 2011." Some things are there in my head, some things aren't.

He's not looking at the monitors anymore. He's focusing in on me.

"Where were you born?"

"Dunno."

"What do you see when you look in people's eyes?"

"Don't tell. Don't ever tell."

"Nothing."

The assistant nearest the monitor says, "Lie," without looking up.

"You heard him, Adam. Let's try telling the truth. What do you see in people's eyes?"

"The black bit, the colored bit, the white bit."

"You see something else."

"Is that a question?"

He's getting really narky now.

"I know you see something else," he says, emphasizing every word. "What is it, Adam?"

We're face-to-face, and he's leaning in even closer now, questions and answers firing back and forth.

"Nothing. Sweet Fuck All."

"Do you see a number, Adam?"

"No."

"Lie, sir."

"Do you see a number?"

"Don't tell."

"No."

"What do you see, you little bastard? What is it? What?" He's losing it now.

Gray-hair steps in. He gets up from his chair and puts a hand on Newsome's arm.

"All right, Newsome. Take five."

"What?" Newsome says.

"Go and cool down."

"I'm fine." He shrugs the hand off.

"It's an order," Gray-hair barks. They're squaring up to each other and there's a moment's silence, then Newsome backs down. He presses his lips together in disapproval and stalks out of the room, gesturing to his assistants to follow, closing the door behind them. So now I'm alone with Gray-hair.

He shuffles his chair forward a little and puts his face close to mine.

"It's OK," he says.

"What?"

"It's OK to tell."

I don't know what to say. If I start a discussion, then I'm giving away that there's something to discuss.

"I know what it's like," he says. "What it's like to be different. To keep secrets. But some secrets are like cancer, they eat away at you. There's no shame in telling that sort of secret."

Have I told anyone? Are the numbers secret? I can't remember. There are big gaps between my childhood—my mum and my nan—and waking up in this place. My mum and my nan are both dead, but what about the girl? The girl I had my arms around, by the fire? I don't know who she was. Or is.

"I can help you, Adam. You want to see Sarah again, don't you? She's here. I can get you back with her, if you cooperate."

Sarah.

Blonde hair and blue eyes. 07252075. Is that Sarah?

"Does she have really blue eyes?" The question blurts out of my mouth before my brain has a chance to stop it.

Gray-hair frowns for a moment, then he sits back in his chair, folds his arms, and smiles.

"Blue eyes? Yes. Yes, she does, my friend. And if you want to see those blue eyes again you'd better start cooperating. It's up to you, Adam. Now, shall I call Newsome back in?"

SARAH

I'm still awake when the cell door opens and breakfast is wheeled in on a trolley. It's the same squaddie who escorted me from the lift to the cell. He doesn't look at me. There's tea, milk, and toast on the trolley. I'm not hungry, but I know we ought to eat.

"I heard . . . things, voices in the corridor last night," I say.

He glances over his shoulder at the open door, then closes it.

"There's a guard out there, for your own security. Maybe they were changing shifts."

Mia's waking up. She opens her eyes and looks around her. She sees the squaddie and ducks down under the covers. I go over to the bed, peel back the sheet, and help her up.

"Good morning, sweetheart," I say brightly. "Do you want something to eat?"

"Where Daddy?"

I look at the squaddie, and then back to Mia.

"He's busy at the moment. How about some milk?"

"Where Daddy?"

"We'll see him later." Then to the squaddie, "Will we?"

"I can't answer that," he says. He won't look me in the eye. "I don't know. I just . . . look after people like you."

Prisoners, he means. How many are there here? Who are they? What was that screaming I heard last night?

"But you know what's going on here, don't you? What sort of place is this?"

He doesn't answer.

"Where are we?" I press him.

He's really uncomfortable now, almost squirming.

"I just bring the meals and work the lift."

And close your eyes to everything else? Is that true? He must know more.

"Is there anything else you need? Mr. . . . . Saul said I had to ask."

"Maybe some smaller clothes for Mia . . . and some bigger ones for me."

He almost smiles, back on more comfortable territory.

"We don't often have children here, but . . . I'll see what I can do."

We're on our second piece of toast when there's another knock on the door.

The squaddie leaves, and Mia instantly turns her face away from the woman that comes in — she's the one who was trying to comfort her yesterday when I arrived.

"Hello again," she says, holding her hand out toward me. "I'm Marion. We got off to a bad start yesterday, but we're going to have a chat this morning." She sounds very sure of herself. She's wearing a sensible skirt, a cardi, and metal-rimmed glasses. I've met her type before, professional busybody, social worker type. Someone like her took Mia away from me once. Someone just like her.

"Not until I've seen Adam," I say, ignoring her hand.

She smiles and smoothes her skirt.

"I don't think that's possible. Let's have our chat and then we'll see, shall we?"

It's not possible. Why? Because he never got here? Because he's dead? Or still unconscious? What isn't she telling me?

"I'm not going anywhere until I know how he is." I fold my arms across my chest, try and draw myself up a bit taller.

"He's fine," she says. "You'll be able to see him later."

"Fine? What does that mean? Have you seen him?

"No, but —"

"So how do you know he's OK?"

"Sarah," she says firmly, "I've been told. I've been told that he's awake and alert, and they're running some tests. Now, do you want to talk here or shall we go to the interview room?"

He's OK. Thank God. My legs are trembling a bit. I don't want that bitch to see, so I turn away from her and crouch down, making a show of attending to Mia, while taking some deep breaths to try and get my feelings under control.

We've got a chance to get out of this cell now, have a look at the place, so I gather up Mia.

"Come on, sweetheart," I say. "Let's go."

Marion ushers us into the corridor and along to the interview room.

It's not what I was expecting. There are leather sofas, a coffee table, a tray with tea and biscuits, and some toys for Mia. They're ordinary enough, the sort of stuff that everyone used to have, but they look like they've come from another age. Plastic cars, a toy phone, a cash register — commonplace things before the Chaos. Things that mean nothing to Mia now. She looks at them and puts them to one side. Then she picks up a doll, a baby that opens its eyes when you sit it up and closes them when you lie it down. She's hooked.

There's a file on the coffee table. Marion sits on one of the sofas, puts the file on her knee, and opens it. What's in the file? Is it about me? Or Adam? I sit on the opposite sofa and cross my arms again.

"So, you and Adam have been together for quite some time."

It's not a question.

"S'pose."

"And you've got one child and one on the way?" She tries to look sympathetic, but I don't want sympathy from her. I pull my top farther down over my bump. "That's going to be difficult for you."

"We'll be all right," I say. "Mia's very good."

"Who do you think she takes after? You or her dad?"

This is dangerous territory, somewhere I don't want to go. Officially, Adam's Mia's dad. That's what I told the nosy social worker who found me living in the squat in London. It was just a spur of the moment thing, but it was easier than telling the truth. Although it's an obvious lie if you stop to think about it—Mia's skin tans a little in the summer, these past two years out in the open, and her hair is curly, almost an Afro, but it's blonde and she's got blue eyes, all the Halligan features, which is what she is. Halligan through and through.

"I don't know," I say. "I don't look for that. She's just her. She's her own person."

"Don't you and Adam play that game? Whose nose? Whose ears?"

"No," I block. "We don't play games."

She must have sussed us, surely, but she doesn't follow it up.

"What about her talents? She's precocious in her speech for

a two-year-old. And it says in my notes that you're an artist — is that something Mia's good at, too?"

An artist. I'd pretty much forgotten that side of me. I haven't picked up a pencil, or a paintbrush, or even a lump of charcoal for two years.

"You painted a mural, a vision of the Chaos, didn't you? That's pretty powerful stuff."

Something else I'm uncomfortable talking about. My dreams, my nightmares — they're best forgotten. I don't want anyone looking inside my head.

"Where did that image come from, Sarah? How did you know what was going to happen?"

"That was two years ago. What's the point of talking about it?"

She puts the file down on the coffee table in front of her. I try to look at it, and she moves it out of my view.

"But it's fascinating, Sarah. You saw the future. You were able to express it. Where did that vision come from?"

"Nowhere."

"Oh, come on. It must have come from somewhere, you didn't just dream it up."

She's got under my skin now. She's pushing me and I want to push back.

"That just shows what you know," I say. "I did dream it up. That's where I got the picture." I'm looking her in the eyes now, defiant. She's sitting on the edge of her chair, leaning forward.

"You had a dream?"

"Yes. The same one, over and over. Every night."

"And you saw Adam and Mia, and the city in ruins and houses in flames?"

"Yes. Yes. All of that, but I don't see it anymore. It's gone. It's past."

"What do you dream now, Sarah?"

"Nothing. My dreams have stopped."

I've lost Mia in this cold and lonely place. I scream her name. . . .

"You don't dream anything at all?"

"That's right."

"And Mia, how does she fit in to this?"

"She doesn't. She's my daughter, that's all."

I want this to stop now.

"What does she see, do you think? Does she see numbers, death dates like her dad? Or visions like you?"

I scoop Mia up from the floor onto my lap. She brings the doll with her.

"Nothing. She's just a baby."

Marion smiles, but it's only her mouth that's moving. Her eyes are cold and searching.

"More than a baby, Sarah. She's a toddler. She can talk. Let's see, shall we? Perhaps she'll draw for us."

She gets up and walks around the coffee table.

"Leave her alone," I say. This is getting out of control. I can cope with questions about me, but Mia's nothing to do with anyone else.

"I'm not touching her."

"You know what I mean."

"Let's try her with these."

Marion reaches into a cupboard and pulls out a stack of paper and some brightly colored crayons.

"Mia," she says. "Can you choose a pretty color and draw me a picture?"

Mia looks at her, makes a face, and buries her head in my shoulder. She still hasn't forgiven Marion for yesterday.

Undaunted, Marion puts the crayons and paper on the floor. Mia peeks sideways at them for a moment, fascinated. Then she slithers down from my lap and kneels by the crayons. Without anyone showing her, she grabs a blue crayon, leans forward so her face is only a few inches from the paper, and starts scribbling. But it's only the first few movements that are uncontrolled. I didn't want this, but I can't help but watch. Marion looks over Mia's shoulder intently.

Within a minute or so, Mia's making deliberate marks, shapes on the paper. She's turned the crayon in her fingers so that instead of gripping it in her fist, she's holding it between her thumb and index finger.

"That's remarkable," Marion says, "for a two-year-old. She must have got it from you."

"She's never seen me draw," I say, and then I realize it's true. For a moment I feel sad, for a part of me that's been lost, and for the childhood that Mia hasn't had.

"It must be innate," Marion says. "From within. She's got it, hasn't she?" She's making notes in her file, scribbling quickly then looking up and studying Mia again, desperate not to miss anything.

I can't tell what she's drawing, but it's definitely something—a shape like a potato with a couple of lines coming out of it. Then she does something else quite deliberate. She looks at the crayons in the plastic envelope, puts the blue one back, and picks out a pink one. Then she traces around the outside of the blue. That crayon goes back and out comes a red one. She draws a similar shape next to the first one.

I lower myself onto the floor next to her. I can't help being fascinated.

"That's lovely, Mia," I say. "What are you drawing?"

She's hunched over the paper, the tip of her tongue sticking out of the corner of her mouth.

"Drawin'," she says. "Me drawin'."

"I know," I say. "It's beautiful. What is it?"

She sits back up on her heels and points to her picture.

"Mummy and Daddy," she says.

I'm the blue and pink potato; Adam's the red one.

A shiver runs down my spine.

She sees us as colors.

Just like Adam's nan.

The first time I met her, Val described my aura, the haze of color I carried with me. I can hear her voice now, harsh and gravelly: *"Lavender, of course, but also dark blue. And all bathed in pink."*

I look at my daughter, and she turns and smiles at me, proud of what she's done. I smile back at her.

"What about Marty and Luke?" As I say their names, a lump rises in my throat. In my head I've got images of Luke clutching his face, Marty in tears. Are they OK?

Mia reaches for the crayons again and draws two more potatoes: one green and yellow, one orange.

If Adam was here, he'd see her number, but I don't need to see it. I know.

02202054.

And she's not just got Val's number.

She's got Val's gift.

ADAM

"For the last time, what do you see when you look in my eyes?"

I look at Newsome, his squashed face, the death in his eyes. Saul's next to him. *Don't ask me what I see in Saul's eyes—I don't know if I could find the words.*

"I see a number." It's the truth. It's the answer to his question, but I feel uneasy saying it.

"Don't tell, Adam. Never tell."

"What does the number mean?"

"It's the date you're going to die."

It's true, but why does this feel so wrong?

"What's my number?"

I stop.

"What's my number?" he repeats.

"Don't tell, Adam. Never tell."

"I don't tell people," I say, echoing the voice in my head. "It's wrong."

"But I'm asking you to. What's my number?"

"I just said, didn't I? I don't tell."

Saul joins in now. "Adam, you're doing this for Sarah, remember? It's all right to tell. It's the right thing to do."

Newsome starts again. "Do you think you're the only one who can see them?"

"No. I dunno. There might be other people but I don't know."

"You're right. Other people do see them. Other people tell, and it's OK." I don't know if this is just a line. Something to make it easier for me to tell him what he wants to know. "What's my number?"

I'm squirming now. They just won't let it go, will they? My body's tense against the restraints, my mind's twisting and turning. I told Saul I'd cooperate for Sarah's sake, I know I don't have any choice . . . but this feels wrong.

"I don't want to say it."

"Just say it."

He's too close to me, right in my face.

"I don't want to."

"Say it."

"I can't."

I want him to back off, but he won't. A fleck of his spit hits my cheek.

"Say it. What's my number? Say it. Say it. Say it."

"11082034."

The fight goes out of me. I sink into the chair, exhausted. My head flops down onto my chest.

"There. Wasn't difficult, was it?"

I don't answer. I got nothing to say.

He's looking back at the screens, running a paper printout though his hands.

"You told the truth. There's no harm in telling the truth. That's what we deal in here—facts, measurements, evidence."

He sounds smug, like he's got the answer to everything. I've just told him when he's going to die and there's no reaction, no human, emotional reaction. He puts down the printout and tucks his hair behind his ears.

"Let's have a few more questions, shall we?"

"No," I say, "I'm done."

"We've only just started."

"Na-ah. I'm done."

"Adam, this is important work. We're trying to save the British nation here. People like you hold the key. We need a generation of strong leaders, people who can establish order, put the country back on its feet, get us back where we should be."

"What's that got to do with me?"

"We need people like you," he says. "You can help us understand the future. We need intelligent early warning systems. Resources are scarce, Adam. We need to know where we can help, where it's not worth our while."

"You don't need me for that. Just walk outside this place and start looking. There are people starving everywhere. Just start somewhere. Do something."

"But what if they're going to die anyway? We can't waste our resources, Adam. It's about targeting them effectively."

"So you want me to tell you where not to bother? Screw that."

Newsome pauses and moves back from me. He looks to Saul, who's sitting quietly, listening intently.

"You can't be emotional about this, Adam," Saul says. "Governments have to make tough decisions."

"I'm not part of the government."

"If you're not with us, you're against us."

The room falls silent.

"We need you to cooperate fully, Adam," Newsome says. "It's important. We need to understand how your gift works. We need you on our side. You could be a huge asset to us. You could be a leader."

"I want to understand, too. Believe me. But why tie me up? Why humiliate me?"

"You killed a boy two years ago. You killed one of our best operatives yesterday. What did you expect?"

That old charge again and a new accusation on top. How many times do I have to tell people? When will they believe me?

"I never killed anyone." I try to sit up, pulling against

the straps, thrust my chin out. What he's saying isn't right. He shouldn't be saying this stuff.

"You lose your temper. You're not in control when you're angry. You're unpredictable."

I twist my head away from him. But he's right. I do lose my temper, and I do lose control. I'm feeling like I could lose it now, if he pushes me any further.

"You've got a choice, Adam. You can help us, support us, be part of something great, something noble. Or you can resist, be stubborn, be childish, and be crushed. Or disappear. You and Sarah. Gone."

There's a long silence.

"What do you mean?"

I know what he means but I want him to say it. I want his bullying and his threats out in the open.

"Who knows where you are now? Who'd miss you?"

The girl. My girl. Sarah. Does she know I'm here? Would she miss me? I can't answer Newsome. I stare at the floor.

I don't like this guy. I don't want him to win.

"Who'll miss *you*?" I say. "11082034 doesn't seem to mean anything to you. Now you know when, but what if you knew *how*?"

That's got him. He stares at me, trying to face me down, but he flicks his tongue across his lips and I know his mouth is dry. I know there's a stab of fear digging him in the guts.

"I see numbers, you're right about that." I look him right in the eyes. "But I feel them as well. And you . . . you're going to suffocate. You're breathing in and out as hard and as fast as you can, but there's no oxygen reaching your lungs. The air's poisoned and every breath makes you weaker, sicker, more confused. You've vomited up everything you've got inside, now you're bringing up bile, but it sticks in your throat and you're choking and fighting for breath, but it's too late. You're on the ground, thrashing about in your own sick. It's over."

There's not a sound in the room.

Saul licks his lips. His eyes are bright, switched on. They're burning into mine. He likes this. Me taunting Newsome. Me describing his death. He's excited.

For a few seconds, Newsome doesn't move. He just looks at me and I look at him. Then he blinks and his hand goes up to tuck his hair behind his ear. He moves away from me, shaking his head.

"Very nice," he says. "A nice party piece. Well done. Did you get that? That piece of storytelling?" he asks the white-coats at the monitors. "What are the readings saying?"

I turn my head. One of the white-coats is holding a printout in his hand.

"Yes, we got it," he says. "Nice even line right the way through."

He looks nervously toward his boss.

"He's telling the truth."

. . .

"Where's Mia?" Marion says. "Where are you in the picture?"

I look up at her. She's still frantically scribbling notes in the file, observing Mia like she was an animal in a zoo. I'm trying not to show anything, but inside I'm totally freaking out. Mia sees the things that Val saw—how mad is that? If Adam was here, he'd see it straightaway. This is something huge, something amazing.

Mia pauses. I know she's wary of Marion, but she's loving drawing.

"Don't stop," I say. "There's someone missing, isn't there? We're not a family without you. Draw you. Draw Mia."

She looks at the crayons and her hand hovers over the packet for ages. Then she looks back at me for help.

"Don't you know what color to pick?" I say.

She shakes her head.

"Just pick any one. Pick a really pretty color." I reach forward and pull out a yellow crayon. "How about this? Yellow, like the sunshine. Like your hair." I hand her the crayon and ruffle her golden curls.

Marion clicks her tongue with disapproval.

"Try not to lead her," she says.

I shoot her a few daggers.

"I'm not leading, I'm helping," I say.

Mia draws a yellow potato next to the first two.

"What else, Mia?" Marion's pushing her now.

Mia puts her crayon down, picks up the paper, and gives it to me. I give her a squeeze and kiss her cheek. "That's beautiful. We can stick it up on the wall, in our room, can't we?"

"I'll take that, if you don't mind."

Before I know it, Marion's snatched the paper out of my hand and has left the room with it. Mia starts wailing and I don't blame her—I can't believe the nerve of the bossy cow. Who takes a child's drawing away like that?

The key turning in the lock reminds me this is not an "interview room." It's another cell. The butterflies in my stomach make me feel sick. I can't do another night in this place. It'll kill me. I've got to get me and Mia out.

"She likes the picture, too," I say to Mia, trying to smooth over the woman's rudeness. "That's nice, isn't it? Do you want to do another one while we're waiting?"

But Mia's tired now. She holds a crayon out toward me.

"Mummy do it," she says.

She picks up the doll and curls up on the sofa. I stroke her hair, and she closes her eyes and puts her thumb in her mouth. There'll be someone else for her to draw soon, a brother or sister.

"Mia, Mia, what does the future hold?" I say it under my breath and it's almost like a song. It's so close that it turns into "Mary, Mary" without even trying.

"'Mary, Mary, quite contrary, how does your garden grow?'

'With silver bells and cockle shells and pretty maids all in a row . . .'"

Her breathing becomes deeper and noisier. She's not asleep but she's very close.

"Mummy do it."

I'm still holding the crayon Mia gave me. Slowly, almost painfully, I take a fresh piece of paper from the pile on the coffee table. I look at the paper for a long time. I'm scared to be faced with such whiteness. There's been no time for creativity in the last two years. Survival's taken over. Now I don't know where to start.

Without really thinking, I begin sketching her shape: the curve of her back, the soft halo of her hair, the profile of her face. Instantly, I'm caught up in it—looking and drawing. Everything else falls away. Part of me's been dead for two years and now, with one sketch, it's alive again. A few lines is all it needs and she's there, on paper. My daughter. My first picture of her. God, I've missed this.

I put the portrait to one side and start making random marks on a fresh sheet of paper. Trying not to engage my mind, I let my hand do what it wants, experimenting with line and form, shading, light and dark. Creating an abstract.

Mia sits up and looks at my picture.

"Whassat?" she says.

I look at what I've drawn and my chest tightens.

The shapes and lines aren't random at all. My "abstract" is a landscape—the light and dark of trees and the spaces between trees. And in the foreground, dark slabs of stone.

"Whassat, Mummy?" Mia asks again.

"Nothing, just patterns," I say, but it's more than that. Much more. It's the place in my head.

The place in my nightmare.

The place where I lose Mia.

ADAM

"That's it, I'm done. You said I could see Sarah. So I wanna see her."

Newsome looks at Saul. I can tell he wants him to say no, but Saul's getting to his feet.

"Yes," he says. "I think that might help."

"Are you sure, Saul?" the doctor says. "There's a lot he hasn't told us. I think we should have another couple of sessions straightaway."

"Newsome, we had a deal. Adam's kept his side. Take those straps off him. I'll take you to her," he says.

"What, now?"

All of a sudden I ain't sure. What if I don't recognize her? What if I make a prat of myself? What if she don't want to see me?

He smiles. "Yes, Adam, now. Can you walk?"

I brace my hands against the arms of the chair and push forward. I'm on my feet but my legs don't feel as if they belong to me. I topple sideways.

"Whoa."

Saul catches me and puts a supporting arm around my shoulders. I'm glad he's caught me, but there's something unnerving about being this close to him. There's a moment when he steadies me and I glance at his face, and our eyes meet and the pain of his death is even stronger, so fierce that it makes me gasp and buckle over.

"We'll get a chair," he says, and nods to one of the white-coats, who scurries out of the room and comes back with a wheelchair.

I look at it with horror. I ain't no cripple.

"I don't *think* so."

"Adam," Saul says, "you came off that motorcycle at forty miles an hour yesterday. You're lucky to be alive. Get in."

He puts pressure on my shoulder, almost forcing me to sit down. My legs give way and I lurch into the chair.

"I'll fetch an orderly," Newsome says.

"No, I'll push him," Saul cuts in.

Newsome looks at him like he's lost his mind.

"What's your problem?" Saul says sharply.

The doctor puts his hands up. "No problem." He turns away, pretending to be busy with his charts and readouts.

Saul wheels me out of the room and into a corridor. I'd assumed I was in hospital, but this ain't like any hospital I've seen before. There are two squaddies outside our door. They make to follow us, but Saul waves them away. They look uneasy, but they do as they're told.

The corridor walls are gray, the floor's concrete. The only people about are soldiers, all in uniform, all armed.

"Where the hell are we?" I ask Saul.

"The safest place in England," he says, but he doesn't explain.

I can hear Newsome's voice in my head now: *"You can help us . . . or disappear."*

"Safe for who?"

"Safe for me, for us. You want to be one of us, don't you?"

I leave his question hanging. I'm pretty sure I don't want to be one of them, but I don't want to rile him, especially not now. I'm vulnerable in this chair. Saul's a powerful man, the man they take orders from in here. And it feels like he's on my side right now. He's helping me. For a moment, I wonder why . . . but there are too many other questions floating around in my head. *That shimmering number, the extreme pain that comes with it, something about it that's wrong . . .*

"Newsome asked me for his number," I say. "But you didn't. Don't you want to know?"

"No," he says. "I don't. "

"I don't blame you," I say. "I wouldn't want to."

"Death doesn't frighten me," he says. "That's for other people."

"That's why I try not to tell anyone. It's like handing them a death sentence."

"Commendable," Saul says. "You don't want to hurt people. I understand that. But it's OK to tell if they ask you and it's OK to tell if you're doing it for the right reasons."

"The right reasons. You mean like I tried to warn people about the quake."

"Exactly. You can help a lot of people, Adam. You should help people. It's your moral duty."

"I don't think it's moral to only help some of them. That don't feel right to me."

"But there's not enough help to go around, Adam. People are going to die anyway, that's one thing we do know. You can reduce the number of deaths if you help us decide who will benefit the most."

My mind's as bruised as my body. I can't argue with him — I ain't got the strength.

"That's too heavy, Saul. It's too much to put on me."

He stops the chair, walks around the side of it, and crouches down, facing me. Is he going to have another go?

"We all carry burdens," he says. "My theory is that we're given what we can cope with, some of us more than others."

His eyes are bright, almost like there's a fire inside him. I've got no choice but to look at him, listen to him. His number dazzles me, skewering me again with its pain. Why does his death hurt so much more than other people's? 02162029. And now I've got another number in my head. 02122029. And a guy lying in the road, a pool of dark blood spreading out around him. Where was that? Who was he? What's the date now?

"And you've been given a very heavy burden, Adam. The power to see death. You can use it. You're strong enough.

I want you to work with me, be my right-hand man. I can help share the strain. I understand, Adam. I do."

He puts his hand on top of mine. "Are you with me, Adam?"

There's something about him that makes me want to say yes. He'd be a powerful friend. And a terrible enemy. But there's something revolting about him, too, something I can't get hold of. My head's spinning.

He can tell I'm confused. He pats my hand and straightens up.

"You don't have to answer now. Think about it. We'll talk again." He looks at the door in front of us. "Do you want to see her now?"

This is it? She's in there? Sarah. My heart starts to thump. My confusion about Saul is pushed to the back of my mind — I'm trying to grasp memories of Sarah. I've got her face, the feel of my hands on her waist as we sit by the fire. But that's all. God, why can't I remember?

No. Not yet. I need time.

"Yeah," I say. "Yeah, I do."

The guard salutes and unlocks the door. Saul disappears inside, shutting the door behind him. My nerves almost get the better of me. Why didn't we go straight in? What's he doing in there? Is Sarah really in there, or is this some sort of setup?

I'm not ready.

But I want to see her — I want to see my girl.

•   •   •

We're back in the sleeping cell. There's a sharp knock on the door, and then the key turns in the lock. I'm starting to hate that sound.

What now? Probably Marion and more stupid questions. I stuff Mia's drawing—at least that horrid cow gave it back— and my nightmare sketch under the mattress. I can't think about it—what it means. I don't want to think. All I need to think about is how to get out of here.

It's not Marion—it's Saul. My stomach lurches. What does he want?

Mia's reaction is even more violent. She lets out a piercing scream, scrambles over the bed, and hurls herself onto the floor. She cowers in the tiny space between the bed and the wall.

"Mia!"

She's got her arms across her face.

"Bad man!" she shouts.

I turn back to look at him. He's closing the door behind him. The room instantly feels closer, even more claustrophobic.

"Where's Adam?" I say.

"Good afternoon to you, too," Saul sneers.

I loathe him. I've never hated someone so much.

"Adam's here. I've brought him from the medical wing."

"Here?"

I try to dodge past him to the door. He steps into my path

and blocks me. He puts his hand up to my shoulder and my flesh creeps where he makes contact.

"A word of warning, Sarah."

"Warning? Are you going to threaten me, because —"

He raises his hand from my shoulder and places his index finger against my mouth.

"Shh," he says.

I jerk my head away, bile rising in my throat.

He smirks. "It's not about you, it's about Adam. He took quite a knock yesterday. There's some memory loss."

"What . . . what does that mean?"

"He's got some gaps, he may not remember much about you, your relationship, the child. You may notice a change in his personality."

I'm scared now. "Are you talking about brain damage?"

He snorts. "Don't be so dramatic. He's had a bump on the head. He's doing very well. Just use your common sense. Don't expect too much."

And then he opens the door.

The first thing I see is the front of a wheelchair. Then Saul wheels him in. I just stand there, rooted to the floor. His face is so bruised and battered, but he's still my Adam. I try to take him in, feeling myself start to melt at the sight of him. Mia doesn't hesitate, though. She's wriggled out of her hiding place and now she streaks past me and flings herself onto Adam's lap.

"Hey! Hey! What's this?" He grasps her shoulders.

Then he shoves her away from him, holding her at arm's length.

"Dad-dee!" she wails, trying to wriggle out of his grip. "Dad-dee, hurt-ing!" She's starting to cry. The tears well up and spill down her face.

The look on his face tells me the awful truth: He doesn't know who she is. And it's like the ground's dropping away. I could never have imagined this happening, but it is.

Then he looks at her, really looks, and his expression changes. He's frowning, almost scowling.

"Nan . . . ?" he whispers.

Oh God, he's seen the number. He's recognized where it came from.

There's a sharp intake of breath from the door. My head whips around to see Saul leaning against the doorframe.

"Like I said," he murmurs, "confused."

But his sharp black eyes are locked onto Adam, and then . . . they switch to Mia. There's a new expression in them I don't like. Something even colder and more calculating than ever. Did he hear what Adam said? Does he know what it means? The way Saul's looking at Mia and Adam, it's setting my teeth on edge.

Mia and Adam . . .

Adam and Mia . . .

Seeing numbers made Adam a target. Does Mia's number-change make her a target, too? Except, no one knows about it but me and Adam.

I need to get Saul out of here, before Adam says anything else.

ADAM

There's a child, a girl. I didn't know there was a child. She throws herself at me, facedown on my legs, hands clawing at me. I feel like I'm under attack. I peel her off me, hold her away. She's only little, I don't want to frighten her, but I don't want her on me—this small, noisy, sticky stranger.

And then I look in her eyes.

They're blue like a summer sky and her number shimmers inside them.

02202054.

It dances in my head and brings the smell of cigarette smoke, the memory of another pair of eyes, eyes so fierce that once they got you, you were caught until she let you go. It's my nan, Val. *What is this?* I don't understand.

"Nan . . . ?"

There's an intake of breath behind me.

And now there are hands on my hands, and another pair of eyes. Just as blue and intense as the child's. But the number's different. It floods me with warmth so every cell in my body glows.

07252075.

"Sarah."

How could I have forgotten? I know her now. I know her story, her past, our life together. I know that she loves me. I know that I love her, and because of our love her leaving will be painless. And I know who this girl is. She's our daughter. She's got a name now—Mia.

Tears of relief well up in my eyes.

"It's all right," Sarah says, and I believe her. Her number tells me that it will be alright in the end. Whatever's going on now, we'll get through it. We'll be together.

"Could you leave us?" she says to Saul. There's an edge to her voice now. Her blue eyes, looking over my shoulder, are hard.

There's a long pause. I don't look at him, just at Sarah. My girl.

"Of course. Take your time. Have a good . . . chat," says Saul eventually.

I hear the door close. A key turns in the lock. There are footsteps in the corridor, growing fainter. He's gone. It's just us.

I look around. We're in a bare cell, three of us shut in together.

I stroke Mia's shoulders with my thumbs. "Mia," I say. "Hello, Mia."

She stops crying and tips her tearstained face up toward mine.

"Daddy," she says between hiccups.

"Yeah, it's Daddy," I say. How could I ever have forgotten? I manage to lift her up so she's sitting on my lap. I wouldn't blame her if she wriggled off and hid from me, but she don't. She snuggles close to me, burrowing in. I try not to wince at the pain. I put my arms around her. She's so little. Her curly hair tickles my chin. I don't know what to say to her, but it don't matter. We just sit and hug each other, while Sarah holds my hand tightly, and watches us with her blue, blue eyes.

"So, how are you?" she says after a long while.

"Sore all over. I can't remember things. Like how I got here."

"What's the last thing you remember?"

"Sitting by a fire with you. There were other people. We were in the woods."

"That was Dan and the people at his camp. Before Saul turned up. So you don't remember him coming, or him taking Mia?"

"He took Mia?"

"Yes. And you don't remember the bikes?"

"Pedal-bikes?"

"No, whopping great motorcycles. That's how you knocked yourself out."

I try to look inside my mind, to search out these missing pages, but I'm grasping at thin air.

"It'll come back." Sarah's soothing me, stroking my hand. "Don't get stressed. You're here now. You're safe, but"—she pauses—"this place isn't, Adam. We've got to get out of here."

"Saul says it's safe."

Sarah makes a face. "What do you know about him, Adam?"

I think about this before I answer. "He's . . . powerful. People listen to him, do what he says. He stopped them asking me questions, got me back here to you."

She looks away from me, examining her fingernails. Then she gazes straight at me again.

"He's a killer, Adam. He shot one of his own men dead, and he shot Daniel in the leg, too."

He shot one of his own men. The guy lying in the road. Is that the killing Newsome accused me of? Why did Saul stay silent? To save his own skin?

I can't say anything for a moment. "No," I say at last. "I can't believe it. . . ."

Then I stop, remembering the dark eyes that seemed lit by fire, the shimmering number. . . .

"I want you to work with me, be my right-hand man. . . ."

Is this the man who abducted my daughter and my girl-friend, who shot my friend? But why did he help me, take my side against Newsome? I struggle back to the present, and then, further back, to the past.

"What happened?"

"It was when we were kidnapped. Daniel tried to help us. . . ."

For a brief moment, I see a man with a beard, standing in the road. A friend. He's holding a rifle to his face, shooting at something. . . . Then the picture's gone.

"I can't remember, Sarah. Why can't I remember?"

I slap my forehead with the palm of my hand.

Mia twists around and looks at me. Her eyes are wide and troubled. She squirms away from me and sits down on the other side of Sarah.

"What else don't I know?" I look at Sarah then, and another memory slots into place—two boys, laughing by the fire. "The boys. Your brothers."

Her eyes fill with tears. "I think they're OK—they're at the camp with Daniel's friends. But I don't know for sure. We have to get back to them."

I feel like I'm going mad. I slap my head again.

"What is this place? Why are we here?"

Slap, slap, slap.

It's not helping. The movement, the noise is winding me up more, but I can't stop.

"Adam! Stop it! Adam!"

I'm shaking my head now, trying to shake my thoughts back into place. I can hear the fear in her voice but I can't stop.

"Adam! Look!"

Sarah's holding something in front of me, breaking through my mad, wound-up state.

"Look at this."

"What is it?"

Peeping around Sarah, Mia's smiling now. "Mia's picture," she says. "Mia done it."

Sarah's smiling, too. "I bet you'll know what it is, if you really look."

There are five round shapes in different colors. Two big shapes—one red, the other blue and pink—and three smaller ones, one green, one orange, and a little yellow one. Straightaway I can see it's a family, a family of shapes. And then I get it, like a thunderbolt striking or a firework going off. It's our family. Me, Sarah, Mia, and the boys.

"It's us," I say. "Did you really draw this?"

Mia nods, beaming, too proud to say anything.

"That's awesome." I put my arm around her and give her a squeeze.

"Adam," Sarah says slowly, "do you remember your nan saying she could see my aura?"

"Daddy," says Mia, pointing to the red shape, then to the blue and pink one. "Mummy."

I look at Mia, and then at the picture again. The colors mean something. I whistle through my front teeth.

"She sees them, don't she?" I say. "She's got it from Nan."

This is big. I can see by the look on Sarah's face she thinks so, too.

"She's got her number, Sarah, and she can see auras, too."

I look down at Mia and her number teases my mind. She's a tiny, fragile little thing, with someone else's number. A death that fitted Nan, but sits oddly with her. She's the living proof that something amazing and terrifying happened two years ago in that fire. I've got goose bumps all over me, and the same question that's nagged at me before resurfaces in my head.

Did Nan give her all this—her life, her gift? Did she give this to my daughter?

Or did Mia take it?

Can she reach out and take anybody's life?

SARAH

"We've got to get her out of here," I say.

"Do they know? Do they know anything about her?"

"No, it's just you and me. But they're interested. There's this woman, Marion, that interviewed us this morning, and she was pushing all the time, poking her nose into our business. She was the one who got Mia drawing."

"Do you think she knew what it meant?"

"No, I don't think so. Adam, we've got to protect Mia. She's special—even more than we thought. She's different."

"Her number's different, too."

"What do you mean?"

"It shimmers in my head. I've only ever seen one other one like it."

"Who?"

He pauses.

"Never mind. You don't have to tell. I don't want to know people's numbers."

He's silent for a moment, looking away from me, toward the door. He's wrestling with something inside, and I know not to push him, so I turn the conversation back to Mia.

"We don't know what really happened in the fire, do we?" I say.

"No."

"Do you . . . do you remember anything that would explain Mia, how she is?"

He rubs a hand over his forehead. I don't want to cause him any more torment, but I've got a feeling that this is important; more than that, it could be dangerous.

"I sent Nan out through the flames," he says hesitantly. "I thought she'd be OK. Her number was a good one. And we stayed to find Mia, you and me."

And in my mind, I'm there with him now. I can hear the crackle of the flames, the splintering of timbers all around us, I can smell our singeing flesh and hair.

"She was hot, wasn't she?" he goes on and his voice trembles a little. "Really hot. We all were. You went out and I held Mia, tried to shield her from the flames. Then I just walked through the fire. I didn't see Nan or nothing."

"I did," I say quietly.

"What?"

I've never told him this before. I risk a glance into his eyes, not sure how he's going to take it.

"Well, I didn't see her," I say, "but I heard her voice. I felt her hand."

He leans toward me and grips my shoulders, hard.

"Why didn't you ever say?"

"I wasn't sure if it really happened. But I think it did. I was confused, disoriented in the fire, but someone grabbed my hand and pulled me around so I was facing the right way. I heard her voice, *'It's this way. Only a few steps more. . . .'*"

He lets go of me and flops back in his wheelchair, staring at me, mouth half open.

"She was there with you. She touched you. So why wasn't it you who got her number?"

"I don't know. My number wasn't that day, was it? Mia's was. Maybe Val reached out to her, too."

I've got tears in my eyes now, and so has he.

"She reached out to you," he repeats. "I never thought . . . I never thought I'd lose her."

"I know. I'm sorry. It feels like my fault somehow. I feel guilty, I don't know why. But we're so lucky to have Mia. It's a miracle we've still got her and we have to protect her, Adam. We have to keep her number secret, keep her safe."

"Yeah, you're right. What she done, what happened to her—it's dynamite. We got to keep it quiet, just you and me. And we gotta get her out of here."

I reach for one of his hands and thread my fingers through his. It feels like we've danced around each other for two years, neither telling the other the whole truth, trying to protect each other, but now we've broken through, and we're both better for it. We're in this together.

And that's when the cell door blasts open.

Light floods in from the corridor as half a dozen soldiers burst in. They don't look at us; they don't speak. Before I can blink, Adam's hand is wrenched from mine as they jerk the wheelchair around and head for the door.

I'm trying to get to him, to drag him back, but there are bodies solidly between me and him, blocking my way. I'm screaming. Mia, too.

"Daddy! Daddy!"

"Adam!"

I'm so focused on him, I don't notice Saul coming in until a deep, sharp voice cuts through the shouting and screaming.

"Take him away."

He's standing there, arms folded, but he's not looking at Adam. He's looking at Mia and me. I can't help thinking about the night by the fire, when he grabbed at her and peered in her eye. I hated him then, and I hate him now. I draw Mia closer to me.

I'm still screaming, but it doesn't make a blind bit of difference. I can't believe I'm losing Adam again. I've only just got him back. I can't believe I'm going to be shut in here.

But that's how it is.

They wheel Adam away, and they all leave, slamming the door behind them.

And then it's just Mia and me once more. Locked in a room

that's five paces by four, with a bathroom that's two paces by three. No windows, if you don't count the peephole in the door. No sunlight. No fresh air.

I lose track of time. Mia's been on a roller coaster today and it's left her disturbed and upset. My mind's churning, but I force myself to calm down, at least on the outside, for Mia's sake, and eventually I manage to soothe her with a cuddle and a song. If only that would work for me, but awake on my own the thoughts spin in my head, around and around.

The same squaddie with the mustache brings food—I've lost track of what meal this is meant to be, too. Soup and crackers. Milk for Mia. And there's something else on the tray— a little plastic cup with a white pill inside.

"I'd take it, if I were you," he says. "You'll get some sleep. Especially after today. We all use them in here."

"No, thanks."

The prospect of another sleepless night is horrific, but I won't take pills.

"Where's Adam? What have they done to him?"

"He's in solitary, that's all I know."

"I don't understand why they took him away. We were just talking. . . . How long will they keep him there? When can I see him?"

He shrugs, but there's pity in his eyes as they flick to Mia, asleep on the bed. "I don't know, I honestly don't."

If Adam's lost to me, then I don't think I can cope. I need him. I love him. Why did it take all this to make me realize?

"I actually have to see you take the pill," the squaddie says, nodding to the plastic cup on the tray. "Otherwise they'll be in with an injection."

I look at him, shocked. He shrugs, but I can tell he doesn't like this.

"I can't," I tell him. "I don't take pills, and anyway, I can't take anything that'll affect the baby."

"They wouldn't give it to you if it wasn't all right."

"You really think so?"

He looks shifty for a minute.

"Shall I put the shower on for you?" he says suddenly.

I frown at him, confused. What's he talking about?

Then he beckons me to the bathroom. I follow him in. He turns the shower on, and we stand next to it.

"We won't be overheard here," he says, keeping his voice low despite the water thundering into the shower tray.

Overheard.

He looks at me steadily, waiting for the penny to drop.

And then it does.

They were listening in. They know about Mia. They know about her number swap and her seeing Val's auras. And they know I want to get out of here. That's why they came to take Adam — to get him out of the way, so there's no one here to protect us. And now I realize, without a shadow of a doubt, that the next person they'll take is Mia.

It means we haven't got long. We've got to escape.

I look at the squaddie. Will the noise of the shower really

block out our words? What if it's a trick to get me to talk more? I have to trust him. I have no choice. He's the only person I can ask, the only person in this place who has shown me any sympathy. "Look, I need your help—we need your help—to get out of here."

I've said it now. What will happen if they've heard? Even if they haven't, I've put my life—and Mia's and Adam's—in this squaddie's hands. For a heart-stopping moment, I wonder if I've misjudged him. Will he help us? We stare at each other for several long seconds.

"It's too difficult," he whispers. "If I'm caught helping you they'll court-martial me."

I allow myself a tiny drop of relief; he's on our side.

"What does that mean?"

He runs his finger across his throat. He looks nervous. If he's acting, he's doing a good job of it.

"Really?" I say.

He nods.

"I'm desperate." I'm close to tears now. "Otherwise I wouldn't ask you."

He bites his lip. He's blinking rapidly, looking at me and then away again.

Then he says, "Adam saved my mother's life." He's talking so quietly I can hardly hear him over the sound of the shower. I lean forward to catch his words. "She had a flat on the twelfth floor of a building in West London. She saw Adam on the TV news and got out. Hers was one of the blocks that went. The whole lot came down. She'd have died if it wasn't for Adam. So I owe him." He looks me straight in the eye. "I'll help you, Sarah. I'll do my best."

"Thank you." I put my hand on his arm.

"I'm Adrian, by the way," he says.

"Thanks, Adrian. Can you get a message to him?"

Adrian sucks the air in between his teeth.

"Please, please," I say. "Wait here."

I run back into the room, grab my sketch from under the mattress and Mia's crayon.

It's difficult to know what to say. Especially if it does fall into the wrong hands. In the end, I write: Come back to me. Trust Adrian. xx

Adam will know what it means.

Then I fold it over twice and hand it to Adrian.

He hesitates, looking at Mia curled up, sleeping, on the bed. He takes the paper and puts it in the chest pocket of his jacket.

Back in the bedroom, he says loudly, "Now let me see you take this. It'll do you good, I promise."

He tips the pill out from the plastic cup onto my hand. I close my fingers around it.

"That's it," he says, giving me a wink. "Down the hatch. Good night, Sarah."

When he's gone, I return to the bathroom and drop the pill into the toilet. It dances in the swirling water when I pull the flush, and then it disappears.

Not long afterward the fluorescent light in the middle of the ceiling goes off and the room is plunged into darkness again, the only light coming from the oblong peephole and the two cracks above and below the door.

I lie next to Mia, thinking of the people I'm missing. Adam, Marty, and Luke. Will Adam get my message? Are Marty and Luke still with Daniel? Is Daniel still alive? All the time I'm thinking, my eyes are open, fixed on the peephole in the door. It's directly opposite the bed. We can be watched all night.

We *will* be watched all night.

I can't lie there, in full view.

I slip out of bed, sidle over to the door. I put my back to it, and slide down on to the floor. I can't see the peephole, and they can't see me. The baby's wriggling around inside me. I put my hand on my stomach and feel something knobbly trace its way from one side to the other; a knee or an elbow. And suddenly it's all so real. There's a new baby in there, another life, and it won't be long until our child is born. What sort of world are we bringing this baby into? I lean my head on the door and close my eyes.

I don't want to sleep, I'm scared of dreaming, but exhaustion washes over me anyway.

• • •

I'm not alone anymore. But it's not Mia with me. It's someone else. His face is close to mine. I can smell his sourness, see the stubble pinpricks on his jaw. He licks his lips, but misses a small bead of saliva at the corner of his mouth. He's breathing almost as fast as I am. I have to get away. I look around for somewhere to hide, somewhere safe. There are hiding places everywhere—trees and stones and bushes. But I can't run.

I can't even walk.

Pain ripples through me, wave upon wave.

My legs won't work. I'm rooted here. Here with him. I've never felt such terror before. I want to scream but my voice is paralyzed, strangled within my pain-wracked body.

Instead, my screams echo around my head. "Help! Help! Won't somebody help me?"

ADAM

I'm in a real prison cell now. Bare concrete walls, a mattress, and a bucket. There are marks on the wall, dark smears. I don't even want to think about what they are.

I need to tell them this is a mistake. I'm not out for trouble. I don't need to be locked up. I didn't even kick off until after they ambushed me, so what the fuck am I here for? I know I didn't help. I lost it again. But I was only defending myself.

My brain won't work in here. I can't figure out what would get me out, how I can get back to Sarah. There must be a way out of here. There *must*.

I don't know how long I've been in here. The lights have

been on the whole time, I've had no food or water. I hear the lock in the door. I sit up on the mattress, trying to be ready for whatever's coming next.

It's Saul.

He nods to the soldier guarding the door. "I'll knock when I'm done."

The door closes, and we're alone.

He leans against the door.

"Adam," he says, "how are you?"

"Tired," I say. *Confused, angry, scared.* "What day is it?"

"Tuesday," he says. I must look blank because he adds, "The thirteenth. February."

The twelfth, the day that guy got shot, was only yesterday. It seems like a year ago. And Saul's number is staring me in the face now. 02162029. Three days to go. And I feel his final pain, like a punch to my guts. It's excruciating, it's obscene to be in that much agony. It makes me feel weak, breathless.

"I want out of here," I say. "I want to get back to Sarah, to Mia. Why did you take me away from them? Why am I here? I don't understand."

He smiles cryptically. "That's what you're here for, Adam. To understand—and to help us understand your gift. We need your help. *I* need your help."

He comes over to the mattress and squats down next to me. I don't like him this close. I shift uncomfortably where I sit.

"I don't want to help if it means choosing who's left to die," I say. "I can't do that. It's not right."

116

"You've got a very simplistic view of right and wrong, Adam. Life isn't black-and-white. It's full of difficult decisions. Sometimes everything's the 'wrong' choice—you have to choose the lesser of two evils."

"I don't believe that. That's twisted."

He shakes his head. "You're so young. How old are you?"

"Seventeen."

The smile fades from his face. "I can hardly remember being seventeen."

He puffs his breath out, looks down at his feet.

"If only you knew . . . ," he says. Then he turns and looks directly at me. I get the full force of his number and it makes me gasp. I want to look away but I can't. He's got me in his headlights. I feel the pain, only three days away now, and I'm terrified. My heart's racing. I don't want him this close. I don't want him in the room.

His number, shimmering. Shimmering like Mia's . . .

Then, finally, I get it. It hits me with the full force of a sledgehammer.

Saul has someone else's number. There's no other explanation.

"You asked if I wanted to know my number," he says softly, watching my face. "But I already know it."

I stare at him. I can't speak. The little muscles in his face are twitching, like the surface of his skin is alive. His black eyes are still burning into mine and deep inside them there's a flicker of madness.

"I've never told anyone," he says, then gives a little laugh. "Well, nobody I wasn't just about to kill."

The hairs on the back of my neck are standing up. Is he going to kill me? Is that what he's saying?

He puts one hand on my shoulder, leans even closer. His breath is sour and there's a bubble of spit in the corner of his mouth. I want to shrug him off, but I can't move. I'm paralyzed with fear.

"I've been looking for you for a long time, Adam Dawson."

"Why?" I ask the question, even though I don't want to hear the answer. My voice sounds far away, tinny.

"Because I want you to be my eyes," he says.

"You what?"

"I want to see what you see. I want to see numbers."

"But I thought . . . Don't you know your own number?"

"I do see them, Adam. But"—he grits his teeth—"I only see them at the very last minute, the very last second." There's an edge of anger in his voice, a hint of the frustration he's bottling up inside. "At the moment when they leave one soul and just before they enter mine."

What?

And then, slowly, painfully, my mind takes the next step.

Them. Saul has taken more than one number.

He's a number-stealer. A cat with nine lives. More than nine . . .

Just like Mia . . .

Just like Mia . . .

I'm riding a motorbike. I feel the wind on my face, the smell of oil in my nostrils, the pulsing of the engine in my hands and legs.

Saul's riding next to me, Sarah on the back. He salutes. A crack, and I'm flying, then nothing . . .

Just like Mia . . .

There's no words to express what I'm feeling—all I can do is sit and stare with my guts turning to water inside me.

SARAH

I wake, wreathed in sweat, to a dark room. I'm lying on the floor. Someone's crying.

Reality's slipping and sliding. Which nightmare am I in?

Am I fourteen again? Is my dad here? The room's dark. There's no lock on the door. I can't keep Him out. Is He here now, or has He just been here? It can't be me crying—I wasn't allowed to make any noise. He said He'd kill me if I did. . . .

Now there's a woman, crouching in front of me. She's got her hand on my shoulder.

And finally, one reality crystallizes from the soup of memories and nightmares. The chemical smell. I remember this chemical smell. My cell.

And Marion. She's silhouetted against the rectangle of light from the half-open door. Her face is in shadow, her body looming over me.

"You were panicking in your sleep," she says. "You were dreaming, weren't you?"

"Get out of my room!" I scream.

"What were you dreaming, Sarah?"

"I don't know. Just get out. Leave me alone!"

But I do know. The panic was real—my heart's still jumping in my chest—and the pain was real and the place was real. I've never been there but I can still smell the dankness in my nostrils, feel the cold seeping into my bones.

Mia's here, too, on the floor next to me—she reaches up to touch my face. Tears brim in my eyes.

"Mummy crying," she says. "Don't cry, Mummy."

But I can't stop. I know there's a time coming when she'll be gone. It's coming soon. I can see it—just as I saw the Chaos. I drew the Chaos without thinking—it was there, in my head. And I drew the new nightmare, too. The dark trees. The stone slabs. The shadows. I've seen it again and I know, just like I knew before—it's going to happen.

"Sarah, what was it? What was in your dream?" Marion's still here.

"Nothing! I don't know. For Christ's sake," I shout, "give me a break!"

"You saw the Chaos, didn't you, Sarah? You saw the date and you drew it. What do you dream now, Sarah?"

"Nothing. I told you already, my dreams have stopped."

"You were dreaming just now. I saw you."

"Was it you looking before? Is that how you get your kicks, looking at people?"

"I don't . . . I don't know what . . ."

"You shouldn't be here, you evil bitch. You shouldn't be in someone's room when they're asleep. It's wrong. This whole place is wrong. Get out! Get out!"

I launch myself at her. My arms are flailing, trying to hit her, scratch her, hurt her.

And finally she moves, hurrying out of the room, slamming the door behind her. Mia's upset again. But she's been through so much in the last couple of days, seen so much.

I take her back to the bed and sit with her until she falls asleep again, maybe an hour later. I watch her chest rise and fall, listen to her regular breathing. After a while, her breathing quickens. Her arms and legs twitch now and again and she murmurs in her sleep.

She's dreaming, too.

ADAM

"I can't help you, Saul. It's wrong. Telling numbers is wrong."

"Where've you got that idea from?"

I clam up. I don't want him dissing my mum. If he did that I really would have to batter him.

He tuts and shakes his head in irritation. "You're not think-ing clearly," he says. "I told you, life isn't black-and-white. I'm acting blind now, I need to know. You can save people, Adam."

"Save them?"

"Save them from me."

I let his words sink in. My mind's reeling now. I thought this was all about the government, all that bullshit about targeting resources, that's why he hunted me down and brought me here. But this is something else. This is personal. I'm here to help one man, this man, a psycho with a mission of his own. Because he means I can save the ones with the wrong numbers, people that are going to die soon—at least, too soon for him. He wants numbers with a long life, and he wants me to find them.

"I just need the right one . . . at the right time," he carries on. It's like he's talking to himself now. "If only I could see num-bers. If I could learn, if I could master it. If I could *pick it up* . . ."

"I can't teach you," I say. "It's something I was born with. I don't even know how I do it."

"No," he says, "you can't teach me. But maybe you can *give* it to me. Would you give it to me . . . if I asked you nicely?" He's smiling at me now, but it's a mockery of a smile, like the grin on a Halloween mask. "I'll give you mine, if you give me yours." He laughs. "Yeah, I like that—it's a swap."

I know then, as clear as day, that if I don't help him, he'll help himself. He'll kill me. In three days' time, when his num-ber is up, he'll take mine and hope my number-seeing comes with it.

"Fuck off, Saul," I say. Fear makes the words catch in my throat. I jump up and stride over to the opposite wall, leaning my hands against it, dropping my head between my arms.

Saul gets up, too. He comes and stands close to me. Too close.

"If not you, Adam, then who?" he says quietly into my ear. "Who's gifted like you? Who's got *your* gift? Your daughter, perhaps?"

Then he walks to the door and knocks to be let out.

•   •   •

Left alone, I've got Saul's words going round and round my head. To be honest, this room ain't big enough for all the thoughts in there right now.

His number's haunting me. I see it shimmering in my head with my eyes open or closed. I can't get away from it.

He's killed more than once to stay alive.

Now he's threatened to kill me.

And he's threatened to kill my daughter.

I know what sort of monster Saul is now. And the worst of it is, Mia has a number that shimmers, too. Nan's number. Does this mean that Mia is the same as Saul? Is my daughter a murderer?

I sit on the mattress and bury my face in my hands. My girl. My little girl. I think of her face the first time I showed her a bird's nest with a clutch of pale blue eggs inside. The wonder on it. The sheer delight.

She can't be a killer, can she?

I don't look up when I hear the door opening again. If it's Saul, I ain't ready to talk no more. I can't give him an answer—well, not the one he wants, anyway. But it's not Saul. It's a soldier carrying a tray of food. A different squaddie every time. He hands it to me and I put it on the bed—soup, crackers, and a cup of water. The guy's still standing there, not moving, almost like he's waiting for a tip.

Finally I look up at his face. He looks the same age as me, a skinny guy with a wispy mustache. He's nervous, a little flushed. He's definitely waiting for something.

He clears his throat, and nods towards the tray meaningfully. I look down. There's something sticking out from underneath the soup bowl.

The soldier turns his back.

It's a piece of paper. I fish it out and unfold it. There's a drawing of a graveyard on one side. Weird. I flip the paper over and there's some writing. Six words: *Come back to me. Trust Adrian.* And two kisses.

It's signed *Sarah*.

"Are you Adrian?" I ask. He nods. "Tell her —" I begin, but he puts a finger to his lips. *Shh.* Of course, they could be listening in. He's clever this one. He knows the ropes.

He holds a stub of a pencil out toward me.

I can send a reply.

I've never been good at reading and writing. I tried, but I never really got it, except now I feel like I could write a book.

124

I've got so much to tell her, so much I need her to know. I want her to know that I love her. I want her to know that I'll get back to her, whatever it takes. I need to warn her about Saul—but I know she hates him already.

Maybe I need to warn her about Mia. . . .

I take the pencil. The soldier makes a show of looking at the paper and closing his eyes. He's telling me he won't look at what I've written. Then he turns his back again.

The end of the pencil hovers above the paper. What do I say? Will this guy really not read the message? What's to stop him having a look as soon as he's out of this room? I would, if I was him. Why has Sarah put her faith in him?

I got a look at his number when he came in—he's got years left, years and years. He's a survivor. But he doesn't look like someone who should survive. There's something weak about him—weak in body and soul. Something doesn't add up. I don't think I want his help.

I write my message. It seems lame.

Trust no one. I'll be back. xx

I fold the paper back up again.

"Thanks," I say, and the soldier turns around, takes the paper, and puts it in his pocket. I nod at him and he leaves.

And I'm left alone with my thoughts again, and with the numbers—Saul's and Mia's—shimmering in front of my eyes.

The light goes on and I hear the key in the door. I've been awake since my nightmare, and now Marion's back.

"Don't come in, you cow!" I shout. "Don't come in here!"

Mia starts to wake up. The door opens, but it's the white-coats this time.

We never had a chance to escape and now it's too late. They've come for us.

Somebody swoops on Mia and picks her up. Half asleep, she starts yelling and struggling. I can't help her. I'm pulled out of bed and my left arm is yanked up behind my back.

"Get off me. Get your filthy hands off me."

I'm pushed across the room and out the door. Mia's gone before me. I can see her hands and feet flailing around, hear her screams.

"What are you doing? What's happening?"

Mia's taken into one room and I'm bundled into another.

The room I'm in has a huge glass window. Through it I can see Mia. She's being put onto a bed. She's fighting them, but they're holding her down, tightening straps around her arms and legs. I can't believe my eyes. It's outrageous.

"Stop it! Stop it! Leave my daughter alone! Leave her alone!"

Someone slaps my face hard, shocking me into silence.

They're taping wires onto her now. It's obscene. What the hell are they doing? She's a little girl, for Chrissake!

A man's standing in front of me now. He's got a white coat on, too, and a squashed kind of face.

"Sarah," he says, "I want you to listen to me."

"Who the hell are you?"

"I'm Dr. Newsome. I'm in charge of Mia's assessment."

"Assessment? What 'assessment'? What are you 'assessing' by treating her like this?"

"We're undertaking a scientific assessment of her extraordinary powers. Someone needs to be in there with her. Do you want it to be you?"

"Yes, yes, of course I do! Tell this idiot to let go of my arm and I'll go in there."

"Good. Let her go."

By the time I've got into Mia's room, they've taped sensors all over her body, including on her scalp.

"Oh my God, Mia!" I rush to her side.

"Mum-meee!"

"It's all right, darling, it's all right."

There's a bank of monitors in the room, a million lights and dials and screens. They're being checked by technicians and supervised by Dr. Newsome.

He leans over Mia.

"Look into my eyes, Mia," he says. "What do you see? Don't worry. You don't have to tell me, just look."

Mia squirms her head away from him.

"There was a little eye contact there. Did you get that?" Newsome asks his assistants.

"Yep, got it," one of them replies.

"Can you turn her around gently," Newsome asks, "so she's looking at you?"

I do as he asks, but only because I don't want him touching her. As soon as we're face-to-face, her features crumple. She tries to reach out toward me.

"Are you getting this?"

"Yes, loud and clear."

"OK, we've got the baseline data," he says. "We're ready."

The technicians start leaving.

"What's happening?"

Newsome turns to face me.

"We'll need to leave you for this part of the procedure. Your role is to stay with Mia, to comfort her."

"What tests are you actually doing? Is it an X-ray? Is that why you're going? She's so young, I don't think you should do that, and I can't be here because of the baby. . . ."

"You'll be fine," he says, and closes the door behind him. I hear a bolt sliding on the other side.

The large rectangle that I know is a window looks like a mirror from this side. All I can see is this grim room, and Mia and me. But I know they're all watching. I feel like an animal in a zoo. I know they can see me and I know they can hear me.

"It's very hot in here," I say, addressing the mirror. "Could you turn the heat down, or put on the air conditioning or something?"

"Yeah, sure," Newsome's voice booms into the room. I glance up—there's a speaker above the mirror, near the ceiling. "We'll sort it out."

Mia's whining, trying to move her arms and legs against the straps.

"Try and lie still a minute," I say. Then, to the mirror, "It's getting hotter."

"There's nothing to be alarmed about. We've got a temporary problem with the heating system. We're working to fix it now."

"Is it hot where you are?"

"Yes, yes, it's the whole system."

"We need some air in here. Can you open the door, please?"

I'm sweating now, and so is Mia. Her forehead is damp and her cheeks are pink. She's only wearing a little T-shirt and underpants.

"Mia's getting too hot," I say. "I'm going to have to take her top off. I'll have to disconnect all the things on her head."

"Sarah, do not touch the sensors. Do you understand me? Do not touch them. We're gathering a crucial set of data that will help with our analysis."

"What analysis? What data? You never actually told me. What are you doing?"

"I'll explain later. Just stay with Mia."

"Is the heat part of the tests?"

"No, there's a fault in the central heating system, I told you. But we must continue the tests. Please sit with Mia."

I do sit on the bed, but not because he's told me to. My legs are starting to feel wobbly. I'm sweating all over and it's hard to breathe. Mia's showing signs of distress, too: thrashing her head from side to side, moaning. The spots of color on her face are getting brighter. I've seen them before. This is getting dangerous.

"What is the temperature in here?" I ask.

"Eighty-six degrees."

"Eighty-six! For God's sake, that's enough. Open the door."

"It's the same everywhere."

"I don't believe you."

Mia's straining at the straps. I touch her face. It's red-hot. I look around the room for some water, anything to cool her down. There's nothing.

"Can you bring us some water please?" I can hear the panic in my voice. I know I should be keeping calm for Mia's sake, but I can't. Alarm bells are screaming through my body. "Dr. Newsome, can you bring us some water?"

"We'll be with you very soon."

"No!" I scream. "We need it now!"

My breathing's out of control now, coming faster and faster, but I'm getting more light-headed.

"Try and keep calm, Sarah."

I look at the bank of monitors near the bed, a battery of traces moving across the screens, with numbers and counters of all sorts. They don't mean a thing to me, except one number. On several of the screens there's the same number: 95 degrees.

I watch as it changes, and, yes, it changes on every screen. 97 degrees. We're being cooked in here.

Mia starts to cry, not a hearty full-on yell like she does if she's fallen over or hurt herself, but a thin, watery noise. Her cheeks were very pink before, now they're mottled—livid red blotches staining her pale, almost alabaster skin.

And I'm back in the burning house with Adam and Mia, feeling the heat from the flames, hearing the timbers splinter and fall around us. We're trapped. The only way out is to walk through the fire. Oh God, oh God, we've got to get out of here.

Mia was moving around a few moments ago, showing her discomfort. Now, she's gone very still. Her eyes are glassy. The changes in her are all happening very, very fast.

"Oh God. Doctor, help us, please. Mia's overheating. Please, help us. *We can't let her overheat.*"

I start scrabbling at the buckles on her straps. I should have done this to start with. I shouldn't have let it go this far.

"Don't touch the straps, Sarah. We'll be right with you. Keep her on the bed. Keep as calm as you can."

"I need to get her out of here."

I've undone the strap around one of her arms, but my sweaty fingers keep slipping on the other buckle and my strength has been sapped by the heat. I can't do it.

"Stay where you are. We'll be right with you."

One more glance at the monitors—106 degrees.

The room's spinning around me. I can't keep it together. I keel over onto the mattress next to Mia. The baby's squirming inside me, pushing against my stomach and my ribs. Saliva floods into my mouth — I'm going to be sick.

I move my head and spit onto the floor. I can't see anymore. The room's gone black. I've got my left arm across Mia. I can feel her even if I can't see her. And I can hear her.

"Mum-meee."

It's a thin, reedy noise, like an alarm bell in my head. It brings me around. I open my eyes and the room comes back into focus. I lift my head just in time to see her eyes roll upward and her limbs go stiff.

"Oh my God. Oh my God. Somebody help us! Help! Please help!"

She starts to convulse, arms and legs twitching against her restraints, head jerking.

I can hardly breathe. I try to hold on to her arms and legs.

"Mia! Mia, come back to me! Mia!"

The jerking gets more violent. It's terrifying, but I can't do anything to stop her. All I can do is watch and try and keep her from harming herself. Then her whole body goes rigid. Her eyes are still open, but I can only see the whites. I cradle her face in my hands.

"Mia. Mia. Can you hear me? Mia. Mia!" It feels like she's gone, like her body's empty. "Oh God, no. Please, please, please." I slap her face. She gives a little moan and her eyes roll down and just for a moment she sees me again, I know she does. "Mia, don't leave me. It's not your time. Mia, stay with me. Stay with me."

·

She's pale now — the blotches have gone — a pale, stick-thin girl lying on a bed much too big for her. Her eyes close and her arms and legs go limp.

The door blasts open, bringing a rush of cold air. Newsome and the whole team of staff sweep in.

"Stand back, please." They jostle me aside and I stagger backward. My body's got no strength left in it. My back hits the wall and I sink to the floor.

I don't know if my daughter's alive or dead.

ADAM

Saul's back. This time he brings a couple of armed thugs with him. Am I going to get a beating? Is he going to kill me now? They cuff my wrists behind my back and shove me out the door. No wheelchair this time: I'm expected to walk.

"Right or wrong, you're going to help me now. You're needed," Saul says, and he barges past and sets off down the corridor at a run. His posse are digging me in the back, pushing me, dragging me along — it's all bruises on top of bruises. I ain't in any position to resist.

"Leave off," I say. "I'm coming, alright?"

My words don't make no difference. They enjoy this shit.

We lose sight of Saul, but it don't take long to catch up with him. We turn a corner and the corridor ahead is full of people running around like headless chickens. They're mostly piling into one room, and that's where we go.

To start with it's difficult to work out what's going on. It looks like there's a crowd of people around a bed, so many I can't see who's on it.

Saul is shouting at Newsome. "What the hell were you doing?"

"I was doing my job, Saul. The girl changed her number—we were scientifically re-creating those conditions to analyze what happens."

The girl. Mia.

They know she changed her number. How? How could they know that? Then I remember the soldier with the message, putting his finger to his lips. *They could be listening in.* They did listen in—they listened to me and Sarah. That's the only way they could know.

What have they done?

"I didn't agree to that," Saul spits out.

"I don't need your sign-off, Saul. I'm Chief Scientific Officer. I sign off on all research. This is my project."

They're facing each other, standing nearly chest to chest like two fighting cocks.

"I'm in charge of this facility!" Saul shouts into Newsome's face. "In charge of the whole damn place! Or are you forgetting that?"

"What do you know about science?" Newsome sneers.

"What do you know about numbers? What are you even doing here?" His chins are quivering.

Saul shoots me a quick look. I twig instantly.

Newsome don't know about his number-stealing.

I open my mouth—I'll shout it from the rooftops if it'll help me get out of here—then I think about Saul's threats. And I remember: He's murdered before.

"If not you, then who?"

I close my mouth. I'm helpless. I can't tell anyone. And anyway, they'd never believe me. My word against his. What can I do?

"What do you know about this girl, Newsome?" Saul's saying. "What has your research shown you? Has her number changed? Or has your scientific meddling killed her?"

Killed her?

I try to shrug off the thugs, to get to the bed. As I twist around I notice a figure slumped on the floor. It's Sarah. I call her name and she looks up. Her face is flushed and shiny, her eyes dull, but they're still that piercing blue and the number's the same. 07252075. Even in the middle of all this madness, her number comforts me. Somehow we're gonna get through this. There's a happy, peaceful, loving future waiting for us. Difficult to believe it, but that's what her number's saying.

And I can't let that number change. I can't let Saul near her. But what about Mia?

"Sarah, are you alright? What happened?"

She shakes her head, unable to speak.

Saul grabs my arm and leads me away from her, pushing through the crowd. Some people protest as they're shoved out of the way. Saul ignores them. And now I can see Mia. Her arms and legs have been strapped to the bed. She's floppy and pale, and completely still. Her eyes are closed.

"For God's sake, what've you bastards done to her?"

"Look in her eyes, Adam. Tell me what you see."

Her chest is rising and falling—shallow little breaths. She's breathing. She's alive.

"Fuck off, Saul. I'm not doing anything until you've untied us both."

"Do it," he says to the people around him.

My hands are wrenched up my back while they fumble with the cuffs, but then, suddenly, they're free. I reach forward, helping the others get the straps and the wires off Mia. She opens her eyes slowly.

Her eyes are bloodshot, but her number's the same. 02202054. Mia's number. Nan's number. It's still there.

Once she's free, I lift her up and carry her over to Sarah. I crouch down on the floor.

"Is she . . . ? Mia, are you all right?"

"Mum-mee."

I put Mia in Sarah's arms.

"So?" Saul's voice cuts in. He's standing right in front of us, looking down.

I close my eyes for a couple of seconds, then glare up at him.

"So what?"

"Has her number changed?"

"I'm not telling you."

One of his heavy boots shifts on the floor—he's itching to kick me, but I'm not in the mood to give in to him.

"For fuck's sake, leave us alone, Saul. We need some space, some time."

"Time," he says, and one of the heavy boots starts tapping on the floor. "We're all running out of time. . . ." His voice sounds strangled and I glance up. His number sears my mind. 02162029. Time really is running out for Saul.

"If you won't tell me, there's another way I can find out," he says. "Give me the girl."

"What does he mean?" Sarah's holding Mia as tight as she can, looking at me for an answer.

I know exactly what he means.

"I do see them, Adam. But I only see them at the very last minute, the very last second. At the moment when they leave one soul and just before they enter mine."

He'll take her away from this room and keep her until the sixeenth, then he'll take her number, just so he can find out what it is. He'll gamble it's better than his own—that her gifts will be more powerful than his—and he won't be wrong. He'll have her number, and she'll have his.

"No!" I shout.

"No?" he says coolly.

"You don't need to do that. It hasn't changed. Her number's the same. They didn't swap."

Behind him, Newsome curses. "Damn! Why didn't it work? We didn't push it far enough. We stopped too early."

"It wasn't her last day," Saul says thoughtfully. "It has to be her last day. She's like . . ." He stops and looks around.

We're all looking at him, Newsome included. I hold my breath. Is his secret out?

"Yes, Saul?" Newsome says. "Like?"

"She's like . . . an angel of death," he says, and as hot as this room is, my blood runs cold.

"How very . . . poetic, Saul," Newsome says, "but we don't know that, do we? I think we should clear the room, continue the experiment. We blinked the first time, so to speak." He looks as mad as Saul now. "This child changed her number—we have to find out what that means, what it means for all of us." His voice trembles with excitement.

"You nearly killed us!" Sarah screams at him. Her voice is high-pitched and piercing. I can hear the terror in it.

"Start setting up the room!" Newsome shouts over her, striding toward the door. "Let's go again."

"No! No, please! Don't do that to us again. Please, please. I'll tell you anything you want to know. I'll do anything —"

Sarah's lost it. Whatever she's been through has pushed her over the edge and beyond.

"What do you want? What do you want from me?"

Newsome stops, his hand on the door handle.

"It's not you, Sarah," Saul says. "It's Mia."

She hugs Mia even tighter. She's shaking, almost convulsing.

"She's just a little girl."

"Does she see numbers, Sarah?"

"No. I don't know. She doesn't even know her numbers yet. She's only two. Anyway, why would she?"

"Because of Adam. Like father, like daughter. Think about it, Sarah. It's important. Do you think she sees numbers?"

"He's not her father, Saul," Sarah sobs. "Not her biological father."

I feel like the ground's tipping underneath me. Another gap in my memory is suddenly filled. Two years ago . . . Sarah was already pregnant when I met her. How could I have forgotten?

Mia's not my daughter.

SARAH

It's gone quiet now, and everyone in the room is looking at us.

"I don't get it," Newsome says. "Why does this matter? We're only interested in the fact that she changed her number, aren't we? She can change. She can renew. She can . . . live forever."

Saul shoots him a look. He's thinking fast, you can see it in his face. His eyes dart from one person to another, and finally end up on me, but he's not looking at my face. He's staring at Mia, cradled in my arms.

"Yes, that's right, Newsome," he murmurs. "But for some reason, she's only done it once. Your experiment didn't work. And she can't see numbers—she's not like Adam. I wanted both—seeing numbers and changing them."

"*You* wanted both?"

"We. I meant *we*," Saul backtracks. "Think of her power, if she has both."

"Do I have to remind you again whose project this is, Saul?" Newsome sniffs. "I've had quite enough of your interference."

I've had enough, too. These people are crazy, out of control, beyond any normal behavior. They don't know what they want—but I do. I want out.

"I've told you what you wanted to know. She can't see numbers. Happy now?" I direct this at Saul. Then I turn to Newsome. "And Saul's right—she changed numbers once. We don't know if she can change again, but you're not putting her through that again. I'm leaving this place, and I'm taking my daughter. Adam, are you with us?"

I turn to Adam, who's crouching next to me. I need him to back me up, stand firm against this unhinged, bickering pair. But he's not listening. I don't think he's heard a single word I've said. He's gazing at Mia, too—and he looks shocked to the core. My stomach goes soft inside. He thought he was her father. It was one piece of the jigsaw his mind had put in the wrong place. He hadn't remembered she wasn't his biological daughter.

I lean closer to him. "You're the only father she's ever

known," I whisper. "You're the best father she could have."

He doesn't react. I squeeze his arm, but he just keeps sitting there, stunned.

I get my feet under me, and heave myself up. It's a huge effort. The baby inside me feels heavier than ever. The bump is sitting lower in my body. It feels like it's pressing on the top of my legs. Once I'm up, I lean against the wall. I've got no strength at all. I close my eyes for a second and breathe, trying to get a little energy into my bones.

I hear a voice. Newsome's.

"And so," he says, "we continue."

I squeeze my eyes tighter shut. I want this nightmare to stop.

"No." It's Saul's voice. "No, it stops here for today. They've been through enough."

I open my eyes. Newsome's squashed face is a picture of angry confusion—and then Saul turns away from me toward him, mouthing something. Newsome's face darkens, but he stops spluttering and sweeps out of the room.

Saul is footsteps away from me now. He moves forward, his hand outstretched. He touches my stomach.

I'm horrified. This guy's given me nothing but the creeps ever since I first saw him. I've hated him from the moment he pried Mia's eye open when she was hiding in my arms. But my back's against the wall—I've got nowhere to go. I stare at his hand. I can't stand it, can't stand the contact.

"Get off me," I snarl.

"Sarah," he says softly, "you must be exhausted."

Adam's on his feet now. He puts his hand on top of Saul's and his fingers shake as they try to peel Saul's away.

"Take your hand off of her," he says.

For a second Saul's hand grips a little tighter and I'm ready to scream, but then he drops it to his side. Immediately I turn and reach out for Mia. She clambers onto me. My knees nearly buckle with her weight.

"Let's get you back to your room," Saul says.

"No!"

He looks at me, taken aback at the venom in my voice.

"I don't want to go back there. I just want to get out of here."

He sighs. "And sleep on the ground? In the mud? In the cold? I don't think so. You need a good night's sleep. We'll see how you are in the morning."

Why's he being nice to me? What's he trying to do? My brain can't make the connection between what's already happened, and what's happening now.

"I can't sleep in this place. I just can't."

"Then you need a little something to help you. We can arrange that. Come along." His hand is on my arm now, shepherding me toward the door.

"No, I don't want . . . I don't need anything, just to be out of here . . . Adam? Tell him."

I glance sideways and Adam is bristling with energy. He's twitching—hands, fingers, shoulders, face. I've seen him like this before and I know what's coming next.

"No, Adam, don't. Please don't. They'll take you away again. Please don't!"

But it's too late.

"I said get your hand off of her. Didn't you hear me?"

"Adam!"

His elbow flies back and then his fist flies forward, making sickening contact with Saul's jaw, catching him off guard. Saul reels backward, clutching his face. Now people are grabbing Adam, restraining him, and they're grabbing me, too, and Mia, pulling us out of the room.

Before I know it, I'm back in the place I dread, desperate and facing another long night. But this time it's different.

I've seen what these people are capable of. There are no rules here. There are no human rights. It's all about survival.

ADAM

So Saul wants to see numbers. If he asked me what it was like, I could tell him. I could say what it's been like for me for the last seventeen years.

Looking death in the face every single day.

Feeling people's pain, their suffering.

Knowing I can't meet anyone without being forced to think

about their last moment. Not even a newborn baby.

When he stepped forward and put his hand on Sarah's stomach, I knew what he was thinking. He said it, didn't he? *"If not you, Adam, then who?"* He thought it could be Mia, that's why he was so hyped up when he learned about Newsome's experiment. But the minute he heard Sarah say that Mia wasn't mine, he changed.

He weren't thinking about Mia no more.

Now I know as clear as day that Sarah and our baby are in danger. Real danger. Saul's time is running out. He could grab a random life, but that's not what he wants. He wants to steal a life that don't just give him extra years; he wants extra powers, too.

He's got less than forty-eight hours.

And now he thinks he's found what he wants.

We don't know when the baby's due, but Saul won't wait. He *can't* wait.

Sarah's not stupid, and she's never liked Saul, but she don't know what I know. And my fists didn't leave us any time to talk about it. I should be sorry. Here I am again, locked up. I am sorry, but only that I didn't finish the job properly. Saul's a monster. I should have killed him. I will kill him.

I walk from one side of the cell to the other. Two and a half steps there. Two and a half steps back again. Over and over. Then I drop to the floor and try some push-ups. The bruises hurt, but I grit my teeth and carry on. Fifty, and I'm still fresh. Fifty more, and I start to feel it in my arms. That's better. Fifty more, and I'm sweating.

I want to be tired and I want to stop thinking, but instead of blocking out the thoughts, the exercise gives them a focus. There's nowhere to hide in this cell. I brace my body, push with my arms, but I keep thinking about the people who aren't here. Sarah and Mia, and the danger they're in. Then, Nan and Mum. I don't know where they are. Somewhere? Nowhere? Suddenly, my grief about them, the feeling of missing them, is a physical thing. A pain behind my eyes, a tightening in my stomach.

I rest down on the floor, lie there flat, with my head turned, one cheek on the cold concrete. I'm frantic with terror and it hits me all over again that I'm the only one left of my family. I got no one to turn to for advice. They've gone. Will Adrian help us? I can't help thinking he won't—not in the end.

I'm going to have to do this by myself. If I keep my wits about me, I'll see something, there'll be an opportunity. I just have to stay alert.

There's got to be some way out of here, and I can figure it out. I know I can. I'm going to.

I've got to protect Sarah, get us out of here . . . and kill Saul.

SARAH

Another doctor, a woman, comes to check Mia. Since we got back to the cell she's been pale, silent, and dry-eyed. She lies on the bed, unmoving. In less than two days I've seen her change from a bright, happy little girl to a frightened shell.

The doctor runs through some routine checks.

"Her temperature's fine now. Her heart rate's good. She just needs rest and some TLC."

TLC. I want to spit the letters back in her face. I bite my tongue, but I regret it when she's gone. I should have told her off. What have we got to lose?

Adrian brings us food and drink.

I try to give Mia some milk. She takes hold of the cup, but doesn't drink.

Adrian goes straight into the bathroom and turns on the shower.

"Are you alright?" he whispers underneath the sound of the water. He looks worked up.

I shrug. "They tried to kill us—how do you think we are?"

"I'm sorry. So sorry," he says, and I believe him.

"Is Adam back in solitary? Did you take the note to him, before?" I say. I haven't had a chance to ask him until now.

"Yes," he says, looking away. "But he couldn't reply. Too much surveillance."

"Thanks anyway. Is there any chance we can get out tonight?"

He shakes his head. "I need some time to plan. I'm getting outside help. It won't be long. Another night or two."

That's too long to wait.

"I don't know if I can cope."

"Hang on in there," he says. "I know it's tough. You should rest, you know. You look tired. I can get you a pill . . . ?"

My legs are like jelly and I can feel the bags of skin sagging under my eyes.

"I won't need a pill," I say. I hate the thought of sleeping here, but I can feel exhaustion creeping over me.

• • •

I kick up when I realize where they're taking me the next morning—back to the room with the observation window. It doesn't make any difference what I do or say. The only thing they give in to is my insistence that Mia comes, too. I don't want to let her out of my sight. And if I see people leaving the room, then we're going with them this time—there's no way we're getting shut in here again.

Mia starts to whimper when we get there. I hold her hand firmly, stroking her fingers with my thumb. This morning, though, they don't seem interested in her. They give her crayons and paper again, and soon she's lying on the floor underneath the bed, scribbling away. Their attention is all on me. They're saying they're going to do an ultrasound on the baby. A scan.

I don't want Newsome or any of his cronies anywhere near me or Mia ever again, but a part of me is curious, wanting to see the baby inside me. I never had an ultrasound with Mia. She was my secret. I didn't even have any help with the birth. I thought things were going to be different with this one. Well, they're different, that's for sure—but not in a good way.

And now Newsome is here. I look at him warily.

"Have you had any prenatal care?" he asks.

"Any what?" I snap.

He sighs, trying to keep his temper in check. "Prenatal care. Have you seen a midwife?"

"'Course not. I've been living rough."

Newsome tuts. "You have a responsibility to this child, a duty of care."

That does it. I'm not taking a lecture from him.

"You didn't give a flying fuck about this baby yesterday. You nearly killed us both. And Mia."

He's got enough of a guilty conscience to look embarrassed.

"That was . . . different," he says. "I'm trying to balance medicine and scientific inquiry here. It's not easy."

"My heart bleeds for you," I say, and his face flushes a deeper pink.

"I've never enjoyed sarcasm," he says. "Let's just do this, shall we?"

"Not you," I say. "I don't want you doing it. I want a woman."

"You're in no position to make demands," he starts, and then a voice comes through the speaker. Its deep, sharp tone makes the breath catch in my throat.

"Do what she says, Newsome."

It's Saul.

I can't help glancing toward the mirrored wall. All I see is my own pinched face looking back at me, but I know he's there now.

Behind the mirror.

Watching.

I want to get off the bed and get out of here, but someone's putting a restricting hand on my arm. I look up and there's a woman in a white coat, the same one who checked Mia last night.

"Just lie back, please," she says.

She lifts up my top and squeezes cold, clear jelly onto my stomach. The skin is stretched taut.

"Try and relax," she says. "We'll have a picture soon."

There's a monitor on a trolley next to her. She flicks the screen on and starts pressing a plastic gun-thing onto my skin, sliding it around, pushing and tilting.

"Here we are. There's a hand, the spine. There's the heart. Can you see?"

I crane forward a little, and I can. There's a baby on-screen, its spine curled, arms in front, knees bent, eyes closed, face in profile. Even in the middle of this nightmare, this moment is magical. I so wish Adam were here. He *should* be here to see this. But at least Mia can share it with me.

"Can you see, Mia?"

Mia's out from underneath the bed, standing on tiptoe, peering up at the grainy, black-and-white screen.

"Baby twinkle," she says.

"Yes, the baby will like 'Twinkle, Twinkle.'"

"No," she says, cross. "*Baby* twinkle."

I don't know what she means.

She nods firmly, like she's pleased she's told me, then she goes back underneath the bed with her crayons.

"Any problems?" It's Saul's voice again.

The doctor shakes her head. "Everything seems fine. Dr. Newsome, do we know what the estimated delivery date is? I can't find it on the records."

Newsome's voice cuts in. "That's not important. That'll be all—thank you. I'm coming back in."

The doctor looks up sharply, then at me. She stays by my bedside as Newsome comes back in, but he ushers her out briskly. I struggle up, ready to run if they try to shut us in here again.

Newsome's talking quickly, but I can't make any sense of his words. My brain stopped working after his first couple of sentences: "There's no need to be alarmed but the ultrasound is showing that we need to deliver the baby early. I'll be doing a cesarean tomorrow. . . ."

I watch his mouth open and shut, his lips fold and unfold. At one point he leans forward and puts his hand on top of mine, a gesture of reassurance. I'm too stunned even to push it away. His hair flops forward and it strikes me for the first time that it isn't his. He's wearing a toupee. It's the sort of thing Adam and I could have a good laugh about, but I'm wondering now if I'll ever see Adam again. If he'll ever see his baby, the baby they're planning to cut out of me tomorrow . . .

Eventually, Newsome stops talking.

"I don't understand," I say faintly. "The other doctor said that everything's OK."

"She meant that the fetus — baby — is alive now, but there are other factors here. The way the baby's presenting, the location of the placenta. A cesarean is the safest option."

"Do I have a choice?"

"It's for the best."

The decision's been made for me.

I look down at his hand on mine, sitting there, like a fleshy toad. And it's as if I'm seeing it for the first time. What is it with people around here? Why do they think it's OK to touch me?

I pull my hand away roughly.

"I don't want an operation," I say.

He gets to his feet. "It's for the best," he repeats.

"I don't want this," I say again, trying to make my voice strong.

He pauses by the door, and through the gap I see someone lurking outside in the corridor. Saul, of course.

"I'll see you in the morning," Newsome says. Behind him, Saul's eyes are glittering and dark. He rubs his hands together, then claps Newsome on the back.

The door closes.

ADAM

"I've come to pass on my congratulations."

Saul's back. He's edgy, jittery, but he's also smiling, like the cat that got the cream.

"What for?"

"You're about to become a father. For real this time."

Sarah. She's having the baby. I ignore his dig about Mia, and jump up.

"I gotta be there, Saul. I promised I'd be there."

"Calm down, it's not until tomorrow."

"What? How do you know?"

He's still grinning. He's loving this, telling me stuff I should have been the first to know.

"Because that's when she's having the operation."

"What operation? What's wrong?"

"Nothing's wrong. She's having a cesarean. Nice and clean and safe."

A cesarean? That's when they open the mum up and take the baby out of her stomach, ain't it? They do that when things go wrong.

"Something's the matter and you're not telling me."

"There's nothing the matter, Adam. She's had her scan and everything's looking good. That's the beauty of a cesarean, you can have it exactly when it suits."

When it suits.

When it suits who?

"Who's decided this? Is it the doctors? Or Sarah? Or . . . ?"

He don't answer me.

"I've got to see her. I've got to. I'll do anything, Saul. Anything."

He's leaning on the wall, his arms crossed. He's pretty relaxed considering I thumped him last time I saw him.

"What would you do, Adam? Would you tell me any number I wanted to know? Would you promise to help me find a good one?" He pauses. "Would you give me *your* number?"

"You're asking me things I can't say yes to."

I try to walk away from him, but it ain't easy in a room this size.

"You *could* . . ."

He's laughing. He's enjoying watching me squirm.

"What's Mia's number?" he says.

"I'm not saying."

"What's Sarah's?"

I shake my head. I'm trying really, really hard to work out what I should do now. I need to get back to Sarah. But how?

"Saul, please let me be there," I say slowly, trying to choose my words carefully. "She needs me."

"Perhaps you should have thought about that before you attacked me."

He's right. I should of, but now I'm thinking I should of finished the job. Maybe I'll do it now. Or maybe there's a chance I can turn things around.

"I'm sorry, Saul. I shouldn't have gone for you."

"No," he says, "you shouldn't."

"I was wound up, 'cause of what had just happened to Mia and Sarah."

"That was . . . unfortunate. Newsome overreached

himself. He won't do that again. I've reminded him who's in charge."

"So you make the decisions around here."

"Yes."

"And it's you who's decided that my baby gets born tomorrow."

"That's right."

He's back to looking smug again. I want to wipe that smarmy look off his face. I can't suck up to him anymore.

"Stay away from them. From Sarah and Mia and the baby."

"Empty threats, Adam. Empty threats. I'm the boss. I'll do what I like. . . ."

I launch myself at him, but he's ready. He blocks me and uses my own momentum to throw me onto the floor. I feel stupid, a boy fighting a man.

He's over by the door while I'm still scrambling to get up. It's opened from outside and he's through and out, with one final blow.

"Look at you," he sneers. "Are you really ready to be a father, Adam? I'd feel sorry for the child—if it survived. It's better for everyone this way. A sacrifice for something bigger, something nobler. Don't worry, I'll do it quickly. It'll all be over, almost before it began."

The door slams and I slam into it, hammering my fists on the rusty metal.

"You bastard, Saul! You leave my family alone!"

•   •   •

There's extra food in our room, the covers on the bed have been replaced by a duvet, and there are toys for Mia—it's the box from the interview room

"What's this?" I ask Adrian.

"Saul's orders," he says.

Saul. It all comes back to Saul.

"Why's he doing this? He thought I was something he'd found on the bottom of his shoe before. What's changed?" Adrian doesn't answer. "Nothing's changed for me," I say slowly, hoping he'll pick up on my meaning.

"I'm trying to get everything you've asked for," he says— and then I know we're talking the same language.

We go straight to the bathroom, as Mia sits on the floor, working her way through the box of toys, looking for the dolly.

The shower thunders into action.

"When?" I whisper.

"I'm relying on other people. But could be soon. Could be very soon."

He puts a hand on my shoulder—the contact feels welcome this time.

"Try and rest," he says. "Leave it all to me."

I try not to mind when the door closes this time, taking comfort in knowing that Adrian's on the case.

I get onto the bed and prop myself up on my side, with a pillow cushioning my bump. My stomach's not exactly painful, just really uncomfortable. I watch Mia with her toys. She's found the dolly again and she's busy talking to it, lying it down and standing it up again.

"Baby, twinkle," she says. "Sleep, baby. Ssshhh!"

The baby moves inside me. I hold my hand to the place where a limb is pressing close to the surface, stroking and soothing it.

"Shh," I say, echoing Mia. "Go to sleep now."

I close my eyes.

The baby settles down.

• • •

He's panting like a dog. The bead of saliva swells and bursts, trickling down the side of his chin. He doesn't wipe it off. Instead, he draws a knife. The handle is some sort of bone or horn, the blade is curved. It's a hunting knife.

I don't understand what I've done, why he's like this.

"I'll use it if I have to," he says. "I've done it before."

I believe him, with every cell in my body.

If only I could run. If only there was someone else here. But there isn't. It's me and him. Me and him and his knife.

"Please, please don't."

I'm begging him now.

Begging for my life.

He's not listening. He's staring with the light of madness in his eyes.

• • •

The walls are solid, the floor is concrete, the ventilation hole in the ceiling is the width of my arm and there's a grille bolted into it. The only chance of escape is when people come in and out. And the only people doing that are the ones bringing my food and collecting my tray. Saul hasn't shown his face since he came to taunt me. I haven't seen Sarah's squaddie, either.

I study the soldiers, trying to take in exactly what they do when they venture into my cell. There's always one with a gun outside who unlocks the door, then the one with the food appears, with a hand on each side of the tray. He checks where I am in the room before he comes in, then he sets the tray on my sleeping platform and walks out backward so he's facing me the whole time. The door stays open so the whole business can be observed by the soldier outside with the key, who shuts the door and locks it again.

There's a moment's hesitation when they first open up. That'd be the time to strike. The guy with the tray's got his hands full, so I reckon I could take him fairly easily. The guy with the key won't shoot me if his mate's between him and me, but he'll be ready for me . . . unless I use the tray as a weapon. I could flip it into one guy's face and barge him backward into the other one.

It all depends on speed and surprise.

I'd have one shot at it and one shot only.

I dunno what time it is. I can't tell by the food 'cause it's always the same. I reckon I'll just have to go for it the next time they come in.

I wanna be ready. I perch on the edge of the bed like a coiled spring, but you can't stay in that position for long. I try pacing about, but I'm using up precious energy. I make myself sit down again, try and focus on Sarah, but that's just mental torture. Once I start thinking about what might be happening my mind runs away with me. So I shift my focus to Saul. And when I picture him, with that smug smile, I feel the adrenaline pulsing through my veins. He's the one who's going to get me through this. My need to stop him. My need to protect the people I care about.

I've lost too many people to lose Sarah, too. I love her, and I know she loves me. If that's taken away, I'd have nothing. It's almost impossible to hold on to people once they're gone. I've learnt that the hard way.

I close my eyes and try to remember mum. She's slipping and sliding away from me. I can't get hold of her. And when I finally do, the picture that comes to me isn't the one I want.

• • •

She's propped up in bed, a shadow of who she used to be. Her face has changed shape, her eyes are sunk in her head. She beckons me nearer. I'm scared of how different she is. I clamber carefully onto the bed. I don't want to hurt her with a clumsy elbow or knee. She puts her bony arm around me and rests her head on top of mine. Her breath smells, like she's breathing out all the chemicals they've been pumping into her. I'm tense and twitchy.

"What is it, Adam? What's wrong? You're a bundle of nerves."

What's wrong? My world's falling apart. You're ill, Mum. You're dying, but no one will say it.

"Nothing."

"Relax. Think of something lovely. Where would you like to be right now? Where shall we go, the two of us?"

For a second I can't think. Truth is, I don't want to be anywhere with her like this. I'd rather go back in time—to when she was just a mum like anyone else's, before she got sick. Except she wasn't ever like anyone else's mum: She was always funnier and crazier and better.

"Let's go to the beach, Mum."

Weston Beach is only a quarter of a mile down the road from our flat. It might as well be the other side of the world— Mum's not able to get out of bed at the moment, let alone stroll along to the boardwalk.

"Is it sunny, Adam?"

"Yeah, but not too hot."

"Fancy an ice-cream cone?"

"In a bit, let's go on the beach first. I want a swim."

"About half a mile to bloody walk, then. . . ."

"We're not walking, Mum, we're running."

"Right, I'll beat you there. . . ."

"No way! I'm already miles ahead."

"Wait for me, then. Hold my hand. . . ."

"No, you've got to catch me. . . ."

We run across the flat sand toward a line of gleaming silver breaking almost silently onto the shore. I slow down on purpose until she grabs my shoulder—"Caught you!"—and then we run hand in hand, on and on and on into the sea. . . .

•   •   •

I open my eyes. I'm in a bare cell, alone.

Why did she go? Why did she leave me? I got nothing left of her.

I close my eyes again and I hear her voice and mine mixed up—and we're saying the same words, the ones I read in the letter she wrote to me when she knew she was dying: *"If you start to forget what I looked like, or sounded like, or anything, don't worry. Just remember the love. That's what matters."*

Remember the love. That's what matters.

I've still got her love. No one and nothing could take that away from me. Not even death.

And I've got people who I love now and who love me.

That's what Saul don't understand. He just don't get it. However many lifetimes he's lived through, he hasn't learnt what really matters.

Maybe that makes him more dangerous.

Maybe it makes him vulnerable.

I don't know, but I know that I've got it. I've got love in my life and that's something worth fighting for.

It's worth dying for.

The blade is dull—cold, gray metal. He holds the tip against my skin. But I can't say anything. There's a gag in my mouth, and it's choking me. I'm looking at his eyes, pleading with mine. But his eyes are strangely blank. He's not seeing my terror, not reacting to my fear. It doesn't mean a thing to him.

Don't cut me.

Don't kill me.

"I've done it before . . . ," he says, and I believe him.

God help me.

And then there's a bang. The noise thuds in my ears.

• • •

I open my eyes in time to hear the next explosion. The sound booms down the corridor. The first thing I think of is the Chaos. It's happening again. I look around for Mia. She's awake. An alarm starts ringing.

"Mummy?" she says.

"I don't know what it is," I say. I'm braced for another shock, for the room to turn upside down. There's a racket outside in the corridor, but it's people, clattering past our room, and the alarm shrilling on and on. Then the people are gone.

The explosions start again, more of them this time. They come in groups, two or three, then a pause, then another two or three. The corridor's full again: thudding feet, shouts, people brushing against the walls.

There's so much noise I don't hear the key in the lock, but

suddenly, Adrian's in the room. His uniform isn't buttoned properly and his hair is sticking up.

"Now, Sarah," he says. "It's got to be now. I'll carry Mia. Wrap her up and bring anything warm you can find."

"What's happening? What's all the noise?"

"I can't explain now. We've just got to go."

I wrap Mia's striped blanket around her.

"Where going?" she murmurs.

"To see Daddy," I whisper.

Adrian scoops her up and I dig my old coat out from under the bed. He hesitates in the doorway. Soldiers are hurtling past in a never-ending stream of khaki.

The guard outside our room is still there, though.

"I've got orders to evacuate these two farther away from the entrance," Adrian says to him. "Can you lead the way? We'll head for the medical wing."

The guard doesn't question him. "Prisoner coming through," he barks, and sets off against the flow, expecting others to get out of his way. Adrian and I follow in his slipstream.

I'm having trouble keeping up. The farther I drop behind, the more I'm getting bumped and barged by people coming the other way. I can see Mia's face looking for me over Adrian's shoulder, then she disappears behind a sea of faces.

"Adrian!" I call out.

He checks behind him and stops.

"Wait!" he shouts at our escort, who also stops.

"I'm sorry," I say. "I keep getting a stitch. I can't go very fast."

"It's OK. Go in front of me. We'll go at your pace."

We're nearly at the medical wing when there's another volley of explosions. This time the floor shakes and everyone stops running for a second or two. Then a voice booms along the corridor: "Code 5. Code 5. Entrance 1 is a code 5."

"What does that mean?" I ask Adrian.

"It means this place is in trouble."

Our guard is pushing back past us.

"You all right from here?" he says. "It's a code 5."

"Yes, sure," Adrian says. "You go, we're fine."

The soldier heads off on the double. We watch him go and then Adrian says, "You'd better put that coat on now, get sorted out."

"What's happening, Adrian? I don't want to go to the medical wing."

"We're not," he says. "We're heading to the stores. Come on, keep going this way."

"The stores?"

I'm trying to talk to him as we walk, but I'm puffing with the effort of keeping up.

"It's the only other way out. They start off in a corridor and then go into a network of caves going right through the hill. People have been coming in and out that way since the bunker's been occupied. They get stuff from the stores, medicines, all sorts."

We've turned into a side corridor now.

"This is where I say good-bye," Adrian says, and puts Mia

down. He strokes her cheek. "Bye, sweetheart. Just keep going, Sarah. You'll find the way without me. And there'll be someone to meet you at the other end."

But I'm not ready to let him go yet. Suppose there are more explosions. Suppose Mia gets so frightened she won't walk. I can't carry her in this state.

"Won't you come a bit farther?" I say. "Just a bit. Let me get my breath back."

"OK, but not far. I need to be back at my post before they realize you've gone."

ADAM

The concrete vibrates against my cheek. Once. Twice. Then the noise comes. Two bangs, like car doors slamming.

I sit up. That weren't no car doors.

There are people running down the corridor, officers yelling out orders, an alarm ringing. I lean against the door and listen to the panic outside. After a while the sound of boots on concrete is gone, but the bell keeps on and on and on.

It feels like it's inside my head.

Then the door opens and I'm on my feet, ready to thump whoever's coming in.

"Adam!"

A man calling my name—that's odd. They don't normally speak.

I stay silent, back pressed against the wall next to the door, so he has to come right in to the room to see me.

He's dragging something behind him, hunched over. In army kit, but shorter than most of the squaddies here. And his hair's tied in a ponytail. This ain't no soldier. And the something he's dragging into the cell is a body.

He turns to face me and his face widens to a grin underneath the dirty beard.

"Adam . . . Adam, are you all right?"

"Dan?"

"Let me park this. . . ."

I help him lug the body clear of the door. It's a guard, unconscious.

Dan straightens up, steps over the guard, and pushes the door nearly to. Then he finds me and wraps his arms around me in a man-hug, slapping my back. I hold on to him for a minute, hardly believing he's here.

"I've come to get you out. You ready?"

"God, yeah. Yeah! We got to get Sarah, though. They're after our baby, Dan. It's sick in here, a sick place."

He looks grim. "You can fill me in later. Someone else is helping Sarah, my contact here, my supplier—Adrian. We'll meet them if we're lucky. If not, we'll see them outside."

"I gotta see her."

"Adam, it's under control. Trust me. Put this on."

He hands me an army jacket. The pockets are bulging. I feel inside. There's a knife and a flashlight and stuff in there.

"This isn't going to fool anyone." I point to my face, the face that was on the TV in a million front rooms.

"Tie this scarf around. It'll get you past a first glance. That's all we need. They won't be looking at you—the focus will be somewhere else."

He looks at his watch.

"Let's give it a minute."

"What are we waiting for?"

My answer comes in the form of a massive series of explosions.

Immediately sirens start wailing and there's the sound of running in the corridor again. I hope to God no one sees the cell door is open.

Dan edges toward it, and peers out.

"Let's go. We're running with the herd to start with."

And then we're off, breaking into a jog, soldiers in front of us. Daniel's limping, and then I remember—three days ago Saul shot him in the leg. Must have just been a flesh wound, 'cause it ain't slowing him down much. We run for a few minutes at the back of the pack, then Dan slows, letting the soldiers ease ahead before he darts down a side turning. I follow him, checking over my shoulder. We're OK—no one's behind us.

"Not far now," he says, as I catch up.

"Where we goin'?"

"Same way I came in. Through the back door."

"And Sarah?"

"She'll be there, too. Sooner or later. Try not to worry."

There's another series of explosions and the whole place shakes.

"Fuck! What *is* that?"

"Friends, Adam. Friends. They may get in this time, destroy the place. But even if they don't, it's the perfect diversion."

"I can't believe you're springing me." I put my hand up and he meets it with a high five.

"Believe it, Adam," he says. "I told you—we need you. We couldn't let you disappear. Here we are."

We turn a corner into another corridor.

Halfway down there are three people with their backs to us, a soldier and a woman and a girl. They must have heard us. They spin around. The soldier draws a gun from his belt. Just as he lifts his arm to take aim Sarah shouts, "Adam!" and Mia screams, "Daddeee!"

Adrian relaxes and puts the gun away and I'm running to Sarah and Mia. Sarah looks exhausted, huge rings under her eyes, but they're as blue as ever and they're sparkling now. She puts her hands around my neck and draws me down toward her. Our lips touch and it's as sweet as the first time we ever kissed. I used to worry that she'd get fed up with me. All those thoughts are blown away by the passion that's there now. She still loves me, and I love her, and a thousand words and thoughts pass silently between us even though we only hold each other for a second or two.

Mia's clinging to my legs, begging to be picked up. I keep one arm around Sarah and reach down to Mia.

Sarah looks past me. "Daniel, is that you? You're alive! Oh, thank God. Where are Marty and Luke? Are they safe?"

"They're fine," he says. "You'll see them soon. But we've got to get through these caves first. It's a bit tight in places, but you'll be OK. There are white marks on the wall, you just have to follow them. Here —"

He digs in his pocket and gives Sarah a flashlight.

"Now let's get out of here. Are you coming, too?" he says to Adrian.

"No, Daniel," Adrian says. "I'm staying. What would I do outside? Good luck, though. I'll see you in a couple of months."

"This place might not be here by then."

Another explosion booms through the bunker.

"I'll still be here. Safest place in England. See you."

We start walking away from him down the corridor. At the end of it is a door. It's open.

Dan stops dead. "That's not how I left it," he says in a low voice. "I've got a key. I locked it." We look at each other. "Someone's been in there, or come out. Maybe more of our people have got in, but I don't think that was the plan."

I set Mia down so I can go in with Dan, see what the problem is. But he's already dodging back, running toward Adrian, who's still standing where we left him, leaning against a wall, head tilted to the ceiling, eyes closed.

"Adrian," Dan says, and he jumps out of his skin. "The door's open. Was that you?"

"No," Adrian says, holding both hands up. "I didn't do anything."

"Come and look."

"I've got to get back, Daniel." Even at this distance I can see his face is flushed.

"Dan," I call. "Leave him. Let's just go."

But Dan's pulled a gun on Adrian now. I don't get what's going on—I thought they were mates—but I'm not going to argue with Dan in this mood.

"Adrian's going to go first," he snaps. "Aren't you?" He walks him toward us. As they pass, I can smell the sharp whiff of fear coming from Adrian. There's sweat trickling down the side of his face.

An open door to an unguarded exit. It can't be that easy, can it?

Dan takes the gun away from Adrian's neck and gives him a shove in the back of the ribs with it. Adrian walks into the room.

"It's clear!" he shouts. "There's no one here!"

Daniel follows him slowly, inching in. I let Sarah and Mia go next and bring up the rear.

I freeze.

We all freeze.

The room beyond the door isn't empty. Saul is standing in front of Daniel and Adrian, and he's holding a revolver.

"Welcome," he says. "Do come in, all of you. Come in and shut the door."

SARAH

I turn around and grab the edge of the door. It's a huge, thick wooden thing, with rivets and old-fashioned locks. Soundproof. As I swing it shut, Adam suddenly lunges toward Adrian. He twists one of his arms and pulls it up his back, making him squeal. Then he reaches into his pocket, draws out a knife, and holds it at Adrian's neck.

"Adam, stop it! Stop it!" I scream, but Adam's holding him tight and he's not letting go.

Dan's standing next to them. His gun is still in his hand. He's aiming at Saul.

"Sarah," he says, turning his head my way and speaking through gritted teeth, "start running. We'll catch up."

Adam yanks Adrian's arm farther up his back. "You knew," he says thickly. "You ratted on us."

I squeeze Mia's hand and start edging behind Adam, Adrian, and Dan.

"I'm s-s-sorry." Adrian can only just get the words out. His voice is staccato with fear. "I d-d-didn't have a-a-a choice."

Adam digs the knife tip in deeper. It's not breaking the skin. Yet.

Mia and I are past them now and, keeping our backs to the wall, we sidle farther into the cave.

"I don't want to hear your excuses. You betrayed us. Your mate Dan. Sarah and me. Even Mia."

"Put the knife down, Adam," Saul cuts in. "You know you're not going to use it. Sarah, stay where you are."

"Keep moving, Sarah," Adam says. "I will use it, Saul. I'll kill him if I have to, and I'll kill you, too."

This is an Adam I haven't seen before. I've seen him hit people in a temper. I've seen him throw objects around and smash things up, but I never thought I'd see him threaten someone with a knife. Looking at him now—with the hatred in his eyes, the sinews in his hand taut like violin strings, the vein in his neck pulsing with anger—I'm not sure he won't use it.

It's frightening seeing him like this, but there's something noble about him, too. He's defending Mia and me. He'll fight to the death for us. I can't tell what's going to happen next, but I don't want Mia to see any more. I ignore Saul and keep moving. We're maybe ten feet away from them now.

"Go on, then," Saul says. "Kill him."

"What?"

"Kill him."

Adrian squeals again, a sound of sheer animal terror.

"You want me to kill him," Adam says.

"I don't particularly want you to. It doesn't bother me one way or the other. I just want this sideshow to be over with. Get rid of him. Get rid of the hippie with the six-shooter as well. Then it's me and you."

It's silent for an achingly long time, silent apart from the sound of Mia and me shuffling along on the uneven stone floor and Adrian, panting like a dog, his breathing fast and loud.

Then Adam speaks.

"I can't do it," he says. "You're right, Saul, I can't do it."

"Let him go, then."

Adam moves the knife away from Adrian's throat. Adrian staggers forward, arms flailing.

"You can't, but I can," Saul says. "This is how you do it." Still aiming the gun at Daniel, he squeezes the trigger.

It's only a tiny movement, but the earsplitting blast fills the cave, echoing off the walls. Dan's gun flies out of his hand. He bends over, clutching his wrist.

I put my hand over Mia's eyes and I start running, dragging her with me. I glance back.

Saul moves the gun toward Adrian.

There's another gunshot, and another.

Adrian convulses where he stands, and then folds forward.

I race deeper into the cave. I don't look back anymore. I can't.

I follow the line of the rock wall, past the first white mark and on and on and on.

Adrian and Dan are both down. Adrian's lying on the floor, face in the dirt. Dan's crouching on his haunches, squeezing his wrist, trying to stop the flow of blood.

"Gun beats knife," Saul says, his voice as cold as ice. "Put it down, Adam, before you do yourself some harm."

I drop the knife.

"Now take the hippie's belt off."

"What?"

"Just do it."

I duck down next to Daniel, undo his belt buckle, and pull the belt out through the loops.

"Sit back-to-back with him," Saul says.

I do what he says. Saul kneels next to us, drops his gun, and grabs my hands. He binds them to Daniel's behind my back with the belt. Daniel yelps as Saul touches his wrist.

"Saul, please. I need to keep hold. I'll bleed to death like this."

"Yes, you will, won't you?" Saul says, carrying on with his task.

He's very close to me. I can see his pulse throbbing in his neck. As soon as he's done here, he's going to be chasing after Sarah. I've failed to stop him. I haven't even bought her much time.

There is a way to save her, though.

I could give Saul what he wants.

"Saul," I say, "you don't need to catch up with Sarah. You don't need to kill my baby."

He tightens the belt until it digs into my skin.

"Oh, but I do," he says.

"You want some more time," I say. "You want to see numbers. You can see them through my eyes. My life, my gift. They're yours, if you promise to leave my family alone. I'll give them to you."

He studies my face, like he was seeing it for the very first time.

"I thought we were the same, Adam, but we're not," he says. "We are different. You'd *give* me your number?"

It's the only thing left to me. I didn't have the guts to kill him when I had the chance. I let my girls down, like I've let them down so many times. I can do this for them, and I will.

"Yes. At least, I wouldn't stop you taking it, however it is that you do it."

"All I need to do is make contact, like this"—he leans forward and grips my shoulders—"look into your eyes and reach inside."

I can't help it. Instinctively I try to look away, but one of his hands switches from my shoulder to my jaw. He forces me to face him. I screw my eyes closed, shutting him out. He laughs and lets go of me, pushing my head away from him.

"You really don't get it, do you? Your baby is everything I've ever dreamed of, Adam. What gifts do you think she'll have? Yours and Sarah's, Mia's, and Val's? She's the product of generations of gifted people. Why do you think your number will do when I can have hers?

"Anyway, I can't kill you. I haven't given up on you yet. Think what we could do if we worked together. You haven't got the stomach for it at the moment, but you're young. You'll learn. We'll be like blood brothers — number brothers."

"Please, Saul. Leave Sarah and the baby alone. I'm begging you. I am begging."

"Like I said, you're young. You've got plenty of time to breed another one, and another. As many as you like."

I've got goose bumps on the back of my neck.

"Stop it. Don't talk like that."

"Like what? Like someone who's lived for two hundred and fifty years? Like someone who knows the score?"

"No. Like someone who's forgotten how to be human."

"What's being human, Adam?" he says. "It's having intelligence. It's being better than animals. It's being able to outwit nature, to triumph, to persist."

Maybe he's right, in a blinkered sort of way. But he's missing something. Something massive.

"What about love, Saul? What about caring for other people, working together, living together? What about families, neighbors, friends?"

"Not important," he sneers. "People come and go — you find that out when you go down the path I've chosen. No point getting attached if they're going to die after seventy years. Three score and ten is over before it's begun."

"But it's what life's about. You get one chance to get it right. One lifetime to live."

"That's old thinking. I can have as many lives as I like. Go on forever."

"But every time you gain a life, someone else dies."

"That's how it is."

I've known it all along. He's an insanely dangerous man. But for his own warped reasons he's choosing to keep me alive. And if I live, then my baby will die. I can't let it happen. I can't.

I'll have to *make* him kill me.

"You really are stupid, Saul," I say.

He shrinks away from me, almost as if I'd hit him.

"Stupid to think I'd ever help you. I wouldn't lower myself. Never. Ever. And if you leave me here, I'll escape and I'll do everything I can to stop you. I'll tell everyone exactly who you are, what you are, what you've done."

Behind me, Daniel is tugging at my hands, trying to shut me up. He don't know what's at stake. He don't know I have to do this, go further, wind Saul up until he bursts with rage.

"You're the weakest, stupidest person I've ever met. You're beneath contempt. You're —"

He picks up his gun and holds it by the barrel, then he slams the handle into the side of my head. I've just got time to close my eyes as the force of the impact carries me over, dragging Daniel with me. I'm out before we hit the stone.

•   •   •

I keep moving. There are lights at intervals along the path, but the surface under our feet is rock, wet in places, and very uneven. We're managing a slow jog at best. Mia is doing pretty well, but she doesn't have much choice. I've got an iron grip on her hand and I'm pulling her along.

There are boxes and crates piled high to one side of us and solid rock to the other. The ceiling is way above our heads — this place is huge. Just when I start to wonder if we're still on the right track, there's another mark on the rock. They're not obvious — you wouldn't see them if you weren't looking. Each one is like a prize.

Before long I get a sense of the walls closing in. The boxes and crates are only stacked one layer deep and you can see rock behind them. The ceiling's getting lower, too.

And then the lights run out. It looks like we're heading for a blank wall.

"OK, Mia, let's stop for a minute."

I switch the flashlight on and train the beam ahead of us.

It's the end of the stores, but not the end of the path. That carries on through a tunnel of rock about three feet wide and just taller than me. I can hear a murmur of voices behind me. Ahead, there's only a dense blanket of blackness.

"All right," I say, trying to make my voice more confident than I feel, "keep holding my hand, Mia. It's going to be a bit dark here."

"Where Daddy?"

"He's going to catch up with us. Come on."

The roof is getting lower and lower. It's not so bad when I can walk standing up, but soon I have to crouch down, walk with bent legs. Water drips from above us. There are puddles on the floor and then we're walking through a sheet of water half an inch deep, that becomes an inch, then two inches

I daren't think too hard about it or I'll panic. Darkness in front of us, darkness behind us, a million tons of earth and stone above our heads. How long did Adrian say the tunnel was? Did he say? And was it just another lie?

The space gets narrower. I go in front of Mia, but I twist around so I can still hold her hand. She's quiet as a mouse, trotting along, keeping up.

I shine the flashlight ahead and there's a solid wall ten feet in front of us. It's a dead end. What the . . . ?

We've been set up. We're stuck like rats in a trap.

"Stop a minute, Mia," I say, and my voice sounds like it belongs to someone else. I shine the flashlight in front of us, up and down, to the left and right. There's a hole in the rock on the left-hand side, about three feet high, with a white mark above it.

"I think this is it, Mia. I think we go through there."

"Dark, Mummy," she says.

I turn around and give her a proper hug.

"We're nearly there," I say, although I haven't got the foggiest if that's true or not. "You're being very good. Have you still got your blanket?"

"Ah-huh."

"Good girl, try and keep it out of the wet."

The only noise apart from our voices is water dripping into water. I can't hear Adam or Saul anymore. We could be the only people left in the world here. Should we just go back? But there's Saul and his gun, and Adam and his knife. God knows what's happening in that room. *Don't think about it. Keep going.*

"You crouch down, Mia. I'm going to have to go on my hands and knees. I'll go first, shall I? You follow me. Stay close, honey."

I put the flashlight in my mouth and lower myself down on all fours.

The water's ice-cold. It's up to my wrists, soaking my knees and shins and feet, even my poor, stretched stomach. I have to use both my hands to move, so my belly hangs down, unsupported. What on earth is all this doing to the baby?

"It's all right," I say to Mia, to my unborn child, to myself. "We're going to be all right." I wish I believed it.

I crawl forward three feet or so and then I freeze. What if the water gets deeper? What if the tunnel drops away?

My heart's going fast now; I can feel it in my throat and my ears, hammering away. I can't move. I'm paralyzed. I'm not touching the rock above me but I can still sense it, the colossal weight pressing down.

Something barges into my bottom.

"Me not like it here."

Mia. She snaps me out of my panic, and I press on. Time

doesn't seem to exist here, so I start counting under my breath. I can manage a minute like this. One, two, three . . .

At sixty, I promise myself that I can do another minute.

And so we go on.

Mia's right behind me all the time, bumping into me with her head. It'd be irritating in any other circumstance, but every little nudge reminds me why I'm here and spurs me on. I'm doing this to keep her safe.

At two hundred and seventy, the ceiling rises away. I take the flashlight out of my mouth and pull myself up on the wall. My knees are sore, my hands and feet are numb with cold. Mia puts an arm around my legs and leans her head on my thighs.

I gasp clammy air into my lungs. It feels like I've been holding my breath for hours. I lean against the wall and try to calm down.

I shine the flashlight around and I can't believe what I see. We're in an enormous cave, empty apart from a mass of stalactites clinging to the roof and their twins reaching up from the floor. After our cell, after the tunnel, the sense of space is mind-blowing. A vast underground cavity — I've never seen anything like it.

"Wow. Look, Mia."

We stand and gape for a few seconds. Then I play the flashlight beam along the wall, looking for white marks. Sure enough, there's one about fifteen feet in front of us.

"Come on," I say. "We can hold hands now."

The first sign that we're near the surface is a change underfoot. We walk out of the standing water and onto dry rock. Then there's a softening of the darkness, just a hint of something different. The air's changing, too. There's a smoky undercurrent hitting the back of my throat.

"Mia, I think we're nearly there."

"Nearly there," she parrots.

The path starts to slope noticeably upward. We turn a corner and there it is — a soft gray lozenge of light ahead of us.

"This is it. Oh, thank God."

My legs start to shake. I can't turn to jelly now. We've got to get out and find somewhere to rest and hide.

There's a rusty metal gate across the entrance. It's only propped there, though. A padlock dangles open and useless from one of its bars.

Adrian said there'd be people here to meet us, but he lied, didn't he? He said what he had to, to get us into the stores. His betrayal sits like a cold, hard lump in my throat. In my head I see him stroking Mia's cheek. I thought he was on our side. But he sent us into the cave with Saul. How could he do that? I don't understand. I'll never understand.

"Hello?" I call out.

There's no answer. I peer through the makeshift gate, but there's no sign of anyone on the other side. I take hold of it and heave it to one side.

"Come on, Mia."

I pick my way through the gap and Mia follows. Then I slide the gate back in place. We're in the middle of a bramble patch, but the branches by the entrance have been broken back and the ground here is trampled. People have been here, and recently.

I try again.

"Hello?"

Even outside the light is muted. It must still be early, but we've stepped out into a foggy world. Everything's shrouded in a gray haze, the fog mixed up with woodsmoke.

I can't see the sky, but I know it's there. It feels like a huge weight's been lifted off me. I can breathe again, really breathe. The bramble patch is in a sloping field with layers of buildings beyond. I can't see any people. We've got no chance of hiding in an open field, so we'd better make for the cover of the buildings and take it from there.

"Here we go," I say, but Mia's ahead of me. She feels the release from our prison, too. She's taken off and is running through the field, jumping over the molehills, laughing as she runs. "Wait. Wait for me!"

I can't catch her, but it's OK, because she runs in random, crazy circles and comes back to me. Her tongue's hanging out like a little dog's and there's a light in her eyes which has been missing for a long time.

My legs are tired and shaky, but the fresh air gives me new strength. I take Mia's hand and we walk to the edge of the field and on to the cobbled street beyond.

The road slopes down toward the middle of the town. We pick our way over broken cobbles, then follow a path between the houses. There's an empty canal, a concrete channel ten or fif-teen feet deep and ten feet across, and at the bottom of it a metal structure lying at a sad angle, the bridge that used to go across.

We stand on the edge looking down for a moment. This place is so quiet that I hear the whine of the drone even though it's still far in the distance.

Mia's chip. Oh God.

Is there any point running? Is there anywhere we can hide from the spy in the sky?

Daniel's mates in the forest had the right idea: shoot the bloody things down.

I can't give up now, though. I can't just sit and wait to be caught.

"We'll have to go back," I say. "We can't get across this."

I feel a stab of anxiety at backtracking—so much wasted time. But we haven't got any choice. We go up the path again and back along the cobbled street. I can't help glancing at the field we've come from, the trail of dewy footprints we left heading away from the mouth of the tunnel. As I look, a figure appears in the fog. It's too big to be Adam. Someone else has come through after us.

I tug on Mia's hand.

"Run, Mia. Run, run, run!"

•　•　•

The ground's hard beneath me. I can feel the lumps and bumps of the rock through my clothes and part of me relaxes. This isn't flat concrete. We got out. We got out of that prison and we're back under the stars. I reach out for Sarah, and my hand finds hers. I open my eyes. At least, I think I do. I move my eyelids, but it don't make no difference. It's either pitch-black or I've gone blind. Where are we now? On some cliffs? In a cave?

"Sarah?"

My voice echoes back to me, along with someone else's.

"Not Sarah. Daniel."

This ain't the seaside. Where the fuck am I?

"Daniel?"

"We're in the bunker, Adam. You've been out cold. Saul got away."

It all comes back to me. Saul and the gun. Me and the knife. Me blowing it.

"How long's he been gone?"

"About five minutes."

"Shit!"

"I've nearly got out of this belt. Can you tense your wrists, really tense them? I think I'm there."

My hands have gone numb, but I feel a tugging, pulling sensation and then Daniel's free. He sits up and finds the flashlight in my pocket. His hand's a bloody mess.

"I thought he'd killed you for a minute."

"Yeah, you and me both. That's the second time that bastard's shot me." He laughs weakly. "God knows why he hasn't just killed me. I need to stop this bleeding. Might take a while."

"I've gotta go, Dan."

I haul myself up to a sitting position.

"I know. I'll follow you. I'll fix myself up a bit first."

"Can you manage?"

"Yeah, yeah. You get started. He's got five minutes on you, that's all. You can catch them."

Another explosion sets my spine vibrating. This one sounds more like a rumble. A stream of small stones and dust tips down from the ceiling just an arm's length away from us. "Dan, this ain't a great place to be if they're blowing it up."

"No," he says. "I wasn't expecting any more bombs. That's either very good news or very bad. I might go back in there, have a look."

"Just get out, mate."

"There's others in here might need a hand. But you must go after Sarah. Go on, Adam. Go. Follow the white dots. There's a bit where you have to crawl, but it's OK. Keep going. I won't be far behind."

"Right," I say. "I'm out of here. Thanks, Dan. I'll see you later." Though God knows if I will.

I set off, heading away from the door.

Behind me, Dan shouts out, "Have you got your knife? Check Adrian's pockets, Adam."

I double back and go through Adrian's things. He's

unconscious, but still breathing. I remember his number—he'll live. But he don't deserve to. There's a phone, another small flashlight, and some keys in his jacket. I pocket the flashlight and chuck the keys over toward Dan. "Here, you might find a use for these."

Then I leg it. I run past boxes and crates and bottles and buckets. There's so much stuff here—food, medicine, clothes. Stuff that's sat here for two years while outside people have been starving and suffering and freezing.

I can't think about that now. What's in my mind is that Sarah and Mia came this way, saw this, were here minutes ago. I've got to get to them, catch up, but there's one person in between.

Saul.

SARAH

I want to make it a game for her, but I can't. I'm too scared. She nods and a frown creases the space between her eyebrows. She's caught my anxiety. She can feel my terror in the sweat oozing out of me, from my hand to hers. I squeeze her hand even tighter.

"Run, run!" I say and we do, as fast as we can down a big sweeping road and into the city.

There are piles of rubble, streetlights lying at all angles like metal tree trunks, but you can tell it used to be a beautiful place. Parts of it still are. Here and there the buildings remain intact, standing like sound teeth in a mouthful of decay. Still holding hands, we run past a big church with a great arched doorway. The square in front of it is full of tents and makeshift shelters, the sort of refugee camp that sprang up in every city after the Chaos. The sort of place that was meant to make do for a few weeks until we all got back on our feet. Two years later it's the sort of place most people are still living in.

Briefly I think about stopping. Maybe we could stay here, lose ourselves in the crowd. But as we pick our way through, the stench hits me. It smells like a farmyard. Instinctively I look down. The cardboard boxes, the plastic sheets, the wads of newspaper are all sitting in a thin soup of human waste. We're treading in it. It's on our shoes now. I grab the hem of my coat and hold it up to my face.

"Mia," I shout, "do this! Do it with your blanket! Hold it up!"

She doesn't argue. She can smell it herself. Her eyes are watering and red-rimmed.

We're nearly through the camp when I get a stitch. I pull up and gasp as the squeezing pain grips me. I stand still and lean forward, but Mia tugs on my hand.

"Mummy, run," she says.

"In a minute," I say, and my words are no more than a whisper. The pain's nearly taken my breath away.

"Mum-my," Mia whines. She's dancing from foot to foot on the spot. I know she hates it here—I do, too—but right now I can't move.

"I know, I know. Just hang on a minute."

I try to breathe slowly and steadily. The pain eases away, my stomach muscles relax. I let Mia pull me past the last shelters, down the side of the church, and on through the streets. But her foot catches in the trailing edge of her blanket. She stumbles and the blanket falls out of her hand onto the flagstones.

"Mummy!" she wails. Her precious blanket is lying in a puddle, wetness soaking into it, making the blue darker as we watch.

"Oh, Mia, for goodness' sake!"

She's looking at it, dancing from foot to foot again.

"There's no point whining. We'll have to leave it."

"No, Mummy. No, no!" She stops dancing and stamps. She's crying now, flapping her hands about.

"Mia, come on. We haven't got time. . . ."

I try to tug her away, but she digs in her heels so I'm practically dragging her along the ground.

"Mia! Stop it!"

"Mummy. Don't!"

She twists her hand out of mine and starts running away from me.

"Mia, wait!"

She doesn't turn around. She's running helter-skelter down the street, away from the church, away from me. I try to run, too, but I can't manage more than a couple of steps before I get another stitch.

"Mia!"

Her back shouts defiance at me. She's getting farther away. The pavement is cobbled and slippery. The sound of our feet is muffled by the fog. And now that I listen, I realize there's hardly any noise at all. This city has a ghostly feel—it's a place that's had the life sucked out of it. And now I get a tingling in the back of my head, a sense that I'm being followed. Still moving, I look over my shoulder. There's nothing there. All I can see is empty street, before the fog swallows it up.

I look ahead again.

The road's empty.

Where's Mia? Where the hell is she?

I pick up the pace, cradling my stomach with my hands. There's a tall wall running down the right-hand side of the road, with branches reaching over the top. It could be some-one's garden or yard. About halfway along I come to an iron gate. It's open.

I put my hand on the metal latch. It's cold and wet—everything's wet in this fog. Inside I can see bushes and trees and suddenly I'm overcome by a sense of dread.

"No, not here," I mutter to myself.

But she must have gone in here. It's the only place on the street she could have gone.

"Mia!" I shout. "Come back here."

I can't see her. There's a path, with trees on either side of it.

I've seen this before. I've been here. I know this place.

"Mia! Come back!" I'm desperate now as I realize what's happening. Dreams and reality are colliding, like they did before. Like they did in the Chaos.

I reach up to push the gate wider so I can follow her in, but the stitch is back. It's not just in one place now, it's spreading over and under my stomach, aching, squeezing, paralyzing me. It's not a stitch—it's a contraction. Goddammit, I'm in labor. Why now? Why?

I grasp the ironwork of the gate with both hands and lean into it, trying to breathe my way through the pain. I close my eyes for a few seconds.

Breathe. Breathe. You can do this.

My eyes are closed but I can still see trees, layers of dark trunks and stones like sentries in my mind's eye. I can feel the gravel underfoot.

There's a face close to mine.

There's a hand with a knife.

It's my nightmare.

I can't go into this place. It's evil.

The pain lessens a bit, and I open my eyes and look through the gate.

There's no one there.

Mia's gone and I have to go after her.

•　•　•

Breathe, breathe, breathe.

There's been another rockfall, more serious this time. I'm crawling on my hands and knees with my flashlight in my mouth when I feel the vibration and, a second or so later, hear the noise. The boom of the explosion mixes with the rattle of falling stones dropping into water and onto me.

The whole lot could come down. I'd be buried here. I feel like I'm buried already—the air's so full of dust it gets stuck in my throat. My chest's heaving, I'm choking, desperate.

Breathe in through your nose and out through your mouth.

That's what my mum taught me when it got too much for me, when the numbers were crowding in on me. I take the flashlight out of my mouth and cover the bottom of my face with my hand, trying to filter the crap out of the air.

In through your nose, out through your mouth.

The noise dies away. Now there's just the noise of my breath, in and out, in and out, and the sound of my blood thudding in my ears.

Sarah and Mia must have done this, so I can, too.

I put the flashlight back in my mouth and press on, swishing my hands and knees through the freezing water. The beam of the flashlight moves about as I crawl, bouncing crazily on the rock wall next to my face. It makes the whole place feel even smaller. All it picks out is a three-foot-wide circle of rock with a weaker circle outside that. Everything else looks blacker, almost like it don't exist. A couple more minutes and then the bright circle of light isn't near my ear anymore, it's way over to my right, and it's picking up these weird shapes, like teeth sprouting up from the floor. Still on my hands and knees I grab the flashlight and shine it around. The ceiling must be twenty feet high and there are teeth there, too, growing down.

"Christ!"

For a moment my mind plays tricks on me. I'm in a gigantic mouth and the jaws are closing. I try to hold the flashlight steady, concentrate the light on one of the weird shapes. It ain't moving. It's a cave, not a mouth, and I've got to get out of here.

I ease up onto my feet, glad to get out of the water. I can breathe in here. My chest heaves as I suck the air in. Something's different here, not just the space. I can taste smoke on my tongue.

Now that I'm upright and breathing, I can run again. Which way next? There's a white mark on the wall. I start jogging, even though my knees are killing me. This has got to be it, hasn't it? I gotta be near the way out.

And I am. Light filters in from an open entrance. I belt up to it and burst out into the real world again.

There's a metal gate flat on the ground in front of me, like someone shoved it from inside and trampled it underfoot.

It's difficult to work out where I am. It's foggy—a cold, clinging sort of fog. There's brambles all around where the tunnel comes out and then a field, a hillside. I can just make out some shapes below, buildings, a city. And leading down, three sets of footprints in the dew: two following a straight line, one made up of little feet, all over the place.

Sarah and Mia made it out.

But Saul is on their tail.

I set off down the hill at a run.

SARAH

"Mia! Mia!"

My voice reaches out into the fog, which flattens it, deadens it, kills it.

There's no reply. Didn't she hear or is she playing some kind of game?

I shove open the gate, stumble in, and set off along the path Mia must have taken. For ten feet or so it's gravel and trees and grass.

Then other shapes appear among the tree trunks, gray-black oblongs. Gravestones. A creature looms out of the fog, a huge bird or something. I can't make it out for a moment, but as I get nearer I can see it's not an animal and it's not alive. It's a winged figure, an angel on top of a pedestal.

I've got to find Mia and I've got to get her out of here.

The gravel crunches under my feet and I leave the path and walk through and around and over the graves.

I think of the camp we've just walked through, the filth of it. This is where most of those people will end up. How many have been buried here already? Does their sickness lurk in this turf? Does it hang in the droplets of fog that I'm breathing in now?

"Mia!"

I spin around. Everywhere's the same. Gray and black. Trees and stones.

The path leads uphill. I'm puffing now. The fog sticks in my throat and my lungs. It doesn't seem to have enough oxygen in it. Oh God, where's Mia? I can't do this. I'm too big, too slow, too tired.

Ahead of me, I catch a movement. Something darting behind a gravestone.

"Mia, I can see you. Stay there. I'm coming."

I struggle up the hill, but when I get to the stone, she's not there. Something low and dark flashes away from me, visible now and then between the grave markers. Quick and silent. A rat.

"Mia! Mia, please, I'm frightened. Where are you?"

Farther down the hill, back the way I've come, something's moving in the mist. Was she down there all the time? Did I plow my way past her?

"Mia?"

The shape disappears again, crouching low, ducking behind a tree. Then a thin voice reaches me.

"I'm here, Mummy."

High-pitched, childlike.

Mia?

My hormone-addled brain registers a child who needs a mum. It could be Mia. I want it to be Mia.

"Mia?"

"Mum-my." Two-tone, singsong. A child calling out to its mother.

"I'm here. I'm coming."

I'm close to the spot where I saw the movement. It was too big to be another rat. I look right and left. Water drips from the branches onto the top of my head. A drop trickles down the nape of my neck and I shiver.

"Where are you?" I call out.

There's no reply this time, but something scuffles behind a gravestone in front of me to my left. I walk forward slowly, placing my feet softly on the ground, willing them not to make a noise. I draw level with the stone. There's someone there, two feet sticking out, bigger than a child's feet, in heavy leather boots.

One more step and I can see. Someone sitting on the ground, back against the stone, knees drawn up.

It's not a child.

It's a man.

He turns his head and looks at me. His eyes seem brighter, more piercing than ever. He starts to move his lips.

"Mum-my!"

It chills the blood in my veins. He smiles, mocking me, and I understand now, the thing I can see in his eyes. Maybe it's power, maybe it's magic, but it's something else, too. There's madness there.

"Saul," I say.

He sits up, stretches out his legs.

"Sarah," he says. "On your own?"

If he's after Mia, I won't let him get her.

"Yes," I say. "It's just me."

"Where's that lovely girl?"

Where is she? Keep still, Mia. Stay hidden, wherever you are.

"She's somewhere safe."

He smiles again.

"Somewhere I won't find her?"

"That's right."

He shakes his head.

"Have you forgotten?"

"Forgotten what?"

"She's chipped, Sarah." He moves his hand and shoots his flashlight into my eyes, laughing. "I can send up a couple of drones. I can look for her myself. If I want to."

"I'm not chipped. How did you know I was here?"

"I wasn't far behind, Sarah, and I had your lovely picture to help." He reaches into his pocket and brings out a piece of paper. "So helpful of you to draw me such a strong visual clue." He unfolds it. My note to Adam.

I curse Adrian in my head, and I'm cursing myself, too. I was a fool to trust anyone.

"What's this all about, Saul?"

"We've got business, you and me."

He's playing with the flashlight now, letting the beam pick out the words carved on the neighboring stones:

ELIZA SANSOM, 1893–1911. TAKEN BY ANGELS.

BERNARD MCALLISTER,

DEPARTED THIS WORLD 19TH FEBRUARY 1932.

EMILY BARKER, B. 1854 D. 1943, MUCH LOVED WIFE TO RUPERT,

AND MOTHER TO VIOLET AND ISABEL.

"I've got no business with you, Saul." The ache spreads from my back to my stomach. Another contraction's on its way. I don't want him to see me like this. Hurting. Vulnerable. "I'm going," I say. "Don't follow me."

But I only manage a couple of steps before I'm gasping with the pain.

Saul springs to his feet. He's next to me in a second, putting his arm around my shoulder. My skin crawls.

"It's coming, isn't it?" he whispers.

Breathe. Breathe. Keep breathing.

He's gripping my arms through my coat, pinning them to my sides.

I can't speak. I can't move, either.

The pain eases.

His face is close to mine. I can smell his sourness, see the stubble pinpricks on his jaw. He licks his lips, but misses a small bead of saliva at the corner of his mouth.

The images I see match the pictures in my head. It was Saul. Of course it was Saul.

"Leave me alone," I say. "I'll do this on my own."

"How long?" he says. "How long will it be?"

My breathing's back under control now, but his isn't. He's panting like a dog. The bead of saliva swells and bursts, trickling down the side of his chin. He doesn't wipe it off.

"Five minutes? Ten?"

"I don't know. *I don't know.* An hour maybe."

"An hour. An hour." His eyes flick from side to side. "I don't know if I can wait that long." The tiny muscles in his face are alive, twitching, and this twitchiness seems to be racing through his whole body.

What does he mean?

"Sarah," he says, "an hour is a long time. But I'm here. I'll help you."

I'm trapped; I'm in labor, I can't run anywhere, I can't fight him. I don't want him here, but I can't do a damned thing about it. This is how I felt at home, for years and years. Powerless. My power taken away by a man. Anger surges through me. I never wanted to feel like this again. That's why I left home. I left everything: home, school, my brothers.

"I don't want your fucking help, Saul. I don't want it and I don't want you here. I want you to leave."

Maddeningly, he smiles.

"I'm staying, Sarah. And if that baby's not here in an hour, I'll cut it out of you."

"What?"

He reaches to his waist and draws a knife. The handle looks like some sort of bone or horn. The blade is long, maybe eight inches, and slightly curved. It's a hunting knife.

No, no! "I've done it before."

"I've done it before," he says, running his index finger along the side of the blade, "but I like you, Sarah. I don't want to hurt you. You believe me, don't you?"

I don't know what to say. His madness is written all over his face. I thought he was after Mia, but all the time he had me in his sights, or rather, my baby. Adam knew. That's why he went for Saul when he touched my stomach. Oh God, Adam, where are you?

The ground's dropping away all around me. Nothing's solid. Nothing's real. Nothing's safe.

Another contraction starts. I gasp, and Saul puts his knife away and grips me again.

"Get off me! Get off!"

He backs off.

"Is it coming? Is it coming now?"

I can't answer him. The pain's got me again. I hold on to the nearest gravestone and concentrate on my breath.

Saul's pacing up and down, like a tiger in a cage. I wish *he* was in a cage. I'm scared of him, really scared.

"New life, Sarah. New life."

That's all he says, over and over. *New life. New life. What's that got to do with him?*

He's still pacing.

Then he stops and looks directly at me.

"I haven't got time."

And he reaches up to pull his scarf from around his neck.

"Saul —?"

He springs forward and starts wrapping the scarf around my face. His fingers are in my mouth, forcing it open, stuffing material inside. I twist my head away from him.

"No, Saul. No!"

I spit and cough, but the scarf's there now and he's pulling it tight behind my head.

"Bite on it," he says. "Bite on it if you need to."

He shoves me down onto the grass and draws his knife again.

I scramble with my legs, pushing myself away from him, scraping my back along the ground, but it's hopeless. He catches me easily and sits on my legs.

"Keep still," he says, "this'll hurt less if you keep still."

I'm twelve again. I'm seeing the emptiness in Dad's eyes as He holds me down. They're the same: Dad, Saul. I hate them. I hate them so much. I didn't fight Dad—I was too scared of Him—but I'm fighting now. Fighting for my life. Fighting for the life of my baby.

He comes at me with the knife and I try to grab the blade. I don't feel the cuts. The pain's blotted out by my anger. He pulls the knife from my fingers and comes at me again. Again I block him. He wrenches the blade away and throws it on the ground beside him. Then he scrabbles at his belt buckle and rips his belt out of his trousers. He grabs my wrists and, easing off my legs for a minute, takes them behind me, wraps his belt around them, and ties it in a knot. Then he's back on top of me and the knife's back in his hand.

There's nothing else I can do. The anger's ebbing away now, leaving raw, naked terror in its place.

"Please, Saul, please don't."

My words come out as muffled grunts, but he could read them in my eyes if he was looking. Only he's not looking, not at my face. He's pulled my top up and my pants down, and he's holding the knife to the bare skin of my stomach. He's poised and ready and just for a moment everything is still, almost calm.

I think, *He can't really do this. It isn't happening.*

He stares as another contraction takes hold of me, watching as the skin on my belly tightens. It's more painful lying down and I start to cry, tears trickling from the outside corners of my eyes and into my ears. The pain's changing. There's something else now, the desire to push. The need to push.

He doesn't have to cut me. The baby's coming anyway.

"Saul! Get off me!"

The urgency in my grunts reaches him. He tugs at my gag, pulling it roughly down over my chin.

"What is it?"

"It's coming, the baby's coming now. Please, untie my hands. Let me get on with it."

"It's quicker my way. Easier."

"No, no, it's riskier. You might cut the baby. Let me do it my way. Untie me."

"I'm not untying you. Do you think I'm stupid?"

"For Christ's sake. What do you think I'm going to do? I'm in labor, you stupid bastard!"

Instinctively he raises his hand to slap me, but as he does so, I start breathing heavily, grunting and growling with the pain and the need to push. He stops, hand frozen in midair, and stares, fascinated. He gets off my legs but he doesn't move away. He stands, watching.

I was alone last time, and, God, I wish I was now. No, I wish Adam was here. This isn't how it was meant to be. I can't think about him. I can't think about anything else.

Breathe. Breathe. Breathe. That's all I can do now.

· · ·

The baby's crying. My baby.

Saul's holding the child. His hands are so covered in blood he could be wearing red gloves. Is it blood from the baby or blood from me?

"A girl," he says, talking to himself. "A good, strong girl."

She's got her eyes tight shut, crying her head off.

I want to hold her. I need to.

My hands strain against the belt tying them together. The knot has loosened already and I wriggle one hand free, then the other. I've been lying on them so the feeling's gone. I waggle my fingers, willing the life to come back into them.

I hold my arms forward.

"Saul," I say, "let me hold her."

He looks up then, startled, like he'd forgotten I was even there.

"It's better if you don't," he says. "Easier for you that way."

And then he stands up and starts walking away.

I can't believe it. This can't be happening. I try to move but it's impossible. I'm pinned to the ground with pain. There's a lot of blood, more than when I had Mia. My stomach is still contracting.

"Saul, what are you doing? Where are you going?" He doesn't answer. "She needs me, Saul. She needs her mum. Don't take her." I try to get to my feet, but the world turns red and then black behind my eyes and when I come to I'm lying facedown. I look up and Saul's a hundred feet away. "Saul! Saul! Come back! Please!"

I'm on my hands and knees now, crawling across grass and leaves and gravel. And then another contraction stops me in my tracks. The afterbirth. I'd forgotten about that. The thing that nourished this baby. The thing my body doesn't need anymore. It's coming out, too. I can't fight it. And now I know that I've got no chance of catching up with them.

Saul's taking my baby and I can't stop him. I rest my forehead down on the gravel. I'm too tired, too desperate even to cry.

• • •

ADAM

In the tunnel, I knew where Sarah and Mia had been. I was following in their tracks, even though I couldn't see an actual trail. Out here, it suddenly strikes me that they could be anywhere. There's a whole world out here. I don't think they'd have stayed in the field, but when I start to get into the city, I feel even more hopeless.

I try asking myself what they'd do. Find somewhere nearby to hide, or keep running? Look for a quiet corner, or go where there are people?

Sarah was getting pretty slow on her feet, and Mia's not the best walker in the world, so I figure they'd both run out of steam fairly quickly. They could be in any of these buildings, or tucked away between piles of rubble.

I half-walk, half-run through the ruined streets. You can still see that this place would have been beautiful. The stone is pale, almost like honey. It's got a sort of light of its own, even in the fog.

I'm in Bath. The place where my dad died, fell off a big church and broke his neck. He was fifteen, younger than I am now. Once I'd read about it in the press cuttings Nan kept, I looked it up on the web, saw pictures. Being here feels like an omen — like I've come to a place of death. I don't want anyone else to die here. I want my girls to be alright.

I start running more quickly, jumping over potholes and cracks in the road. There are abandoned cars everywhere.

They could be in one of them. Do I stop and look in each one?

This is useless. I'm like a headless chicken.

I need help. I need other people, people who may have seen them.

There's smoke mixing in with the fog, woodsmoke. It smells like every fire we made when we were camping out together and it fills me with memories of food, company, sitting with my arms around Sarah, watching the flames together until our eyelids went heavy. Fire means people. I follow the smell and come out into a big public square, next to a church.

One half of the church has gone, but the front's still there, a big doorway and a massive wall of stone dotted with holes where the windows used to be. The area in front is a sea of makeshift tents, a refugee city. There are fires going and people picking their way around or just sitting. I scan the scene. What were Sarah and Mia wearing? Is there any way I can spot them in the crowd?

I start weaving my way through. The ground is wet and filthy. These people are sitting in filth. The whole place stinks. I can't imagine Sarah stopping here unless she was desperate. But maybe she was. . . .

I go up to a woman squatting by a fire, heating some water. Her hands are gray with dirt, her hair's all matted and stiff. "'Scuse me," I say. "Have you seen a woman and a little girl, a toddler?"

She looks at me and squints her eyes, like she's trying to work out if she knows me or not. Then she shakes her head.

I carry on, looking at faces, stopping here and there to ask about Sarah. People are watching me now. There's a buzz of talking and I can pick out my name being said. They recognize me. I've cursed my so-called fame for so long, but now I can use it. I've got an audience, if I can get them to listen. . . .

I stand in the middle of the crowd and take a deep breath.

"I'm Adam," I shout.

A few people shout back, "Hello, Adam!" and there's a ripple of applause.

It takes me by surprise. I didn't expect that. I don't know what to do, how to react, so I just stand and listen, waiting until the noise dies down.

"I need your help," I continue. "I'm looking for two people. A woman, not much shorter than me, she's pregnant"—I hold my arms out in front of me to illustrate—"nearly ready to pop. And a little girl. She's only two, got curly blonde hair like a little angel. Are they here? Have you seen them? Has anyone seen them?"

There's a lot of shaking of heads but then a woman's voice pipes up.

"There were two like that. They stopped for a minute, but then they went away."

I spin around to see who's speaking, but at that moment a door opens to the main archway in the church and a man comes out. He's carrying a pair of buckets that steam gently in the cold air. A roar sweeps across the square, and people jump up and charge toward the church. The man sets his buckets down a few steps away from the door and a queue forms as he starts doling out ladles of something hot onto plates and bowls and anything else people bring him.

"Wait! Wait a minute. Who saw her? Who was it?"

Whoever it was is lost in the feeding frenzy. I get swept along in the tide. The guy with the buckets seems to belong here, maybe he'll know something, but I can't get near enough to ask him. I'm trying to push through to him when my foot steps on something soft. I look down. It's a blanket. A blue and white striped blanket, though the blue's wet and dark and the white's gray.

It's Mia's.

She was here.

I'm in one corner of the square and there's a road leading out. They either came in to the square this way or this is where they left it. I leave the queue and head for the exit. No one minds me trying to go this way and I'm soon out of the crowd and onto the side street.

It's empty, a long, straight cobbled road, with the abbey on one side and a long, high wall on the other. The end of the street's lost in fog; I can't see what's beyond.

I start running.

To my right, a branch dangles over the top of the wall, like swollen, knobbly fingers. Trees, I think. Trees in the middle of the city.

There's a gate in the wall, an ancient metal thing. I glance through as I run past. A path leads away from it, with trees and bushes on either side. I've gone another hundred feet before I skid to a halt.

The place behind the gate. I've seen it before, at least I think I have. If I'm right, there should be stones there, too. Gravestones.

SARAH

I'm not alone anymore. There are footsteps. I can hear gravel crunching, feel the vibration through the ground. I'm too tired to open my eyes. I haven't got the strength to lift my head and see who it is.

"What have you done to her, you evil bitch?"

It's Saul. He's back. I force my eyes open. I can see his heavy black boots next to my face. Slowly, I twist around and look up. He's holding the baby at arm's length.

"You're a witch. You've hexed her. She's no good to me and you know it. You knew it all along."

I don't know what he's talking about.

"Give her to me. Please, Saul. Give me my baby."

He reaches forward and I think he's going to hand her to me, but he lets her drop, like a rag doll.

"No!"

I forget my pain; I find some energy from somewhere

and my hands move to meet her. She nearly slips through my wet, bleeding fingers, but somehow I manage to hold on to her and gather her safely into my body. She's naked and very cold.

"Have you got something to wrap her in? Can I have your coat?"

"No, you can't," he spits out. "I've got your mess all over it anyway. Isn't that enough? "

"She's freezing. I have to keep her warm."

"Give her your own coat, then."

I put the baby carefully on the ground next to me and slide out of my coat. I wrap her up, making sure her hands and feet are tucked in. Only the top of her face is showing, eyes closed, not crying anymore. How can she sleep through this, all the noise, being thrown about?

"Hello," I whisper. I want her to open her eyes. I want her to see me and I want to see her. She's so cold now, so still, her eyes so firmly shut. Is it too late for her? Is this her first and last day?

"Is she dying, Saul. Is she dead?"

I look up at him and there's pure venom in his eyes.

"I don't know and I don't care. She's no good to me," he says. "You fixed it so she's no good."

"I didn't. I don't know what you're talking about. . . ."

He crouches down beside us.

"Look at your baby, Sarah. Look at your precious girl. She's no good to me because she has no eyes."

It feels like my stomach's falling away from the rest of me.

He's wrong. He's got to be. I look at her again. She has eyelids. She has eyelashes. I place my thumb above her eye socket and gently pull the skin. There's no gap between the eyelids. Her lashes mark the line where the gap would be, but it's solid. I move my thumb down. The area below is smooth, not rounded. There's no eyeball. Saul's right. My daughter has no eyes.

But her face looks so perfect, round like a little apple. As I hold her, a bit of color is starting to spread into her cheeks. She's warming up. Maybe she's going to be OK.

"I didn't do anything, Saul. I don't know what's happened."

"I don't believe you. But it doesn't matter now. She's no good to me."

"What did you want her for? Why did you do what you did?"

He frowns and looks at me like I'm stupid.

"Her number, Sarah. Her life. There's nothing better than a newborn number. It makes you feel . . . *alive*, really alive. And with Adam as her father, you as her mother, she'd bring me the gift of seeing numbers and who knows what else."

"You wanted to steal her number. You can steal numbers. . . ."

"*Steal* is an unpleasant word. I prefer *swap*."

Swapping numbers. Just like Mia. *Is* he like Mia? Is Mia like *him*? Are they the same? They can't be. My daughter can't be the same as this monster. Can she? And God, where *is* she?

"I thought you wanted Mia," I say dully.

"I did when I thought she had Adam's blood, but that was another one of your lies, another deceit, wasn't it? But I'm running out of time. Today's the day, Sarah, so I'll have to make do . . . with you."

"Why today? Why now?"

"My number's up. I've used up one life. I need another one. Now, sit still."

He fixes me with his eyes, and the bead of saliva is at the corner of his mouth again. He's excited, like he was before the baby was born. I'm completely defenseless. There's nowhere to hide.

He cups my face. His hands are red and sticky from my blood. He spreads his fingers out so he's holding my head still, the heel of his hands at my chin, his fingertips in my hair. He moves his face close. Closer. Closer.

I can see every detail, each pimple and pockmark, each little scar, each pore. I don't want him near me. I don't want him touching me. I close my eyes.

"No, no, Sarah," he says, and his voice is no more than a whisper. "No, no, I'll need your eyes open."

I clamp them tighter shut. "Open your eyes. Open them!"

I'm in pain, defenseless, but not defeated yet. There's still a remnant of the old Sarah; the Sarah who left home and made a new life for herself; the Sarah who struggled and kept three kids alive through two harsh winters.

"No," I say keeping my eyelids closed tight. "Fuck off, Saul. Fuck off and leave me alone."

He snarls like an animal and then moves his hands on my face, pressing his thumbs into the skin above my eyelids, forcing them open. He's only a few inches away.

"Look at me, Sarah. Look at me."

His eyes are locked into mine. His pupils are dilated, obscuring his irises. His eyes are just black and white now, and however much I want to look away, I can't. I look into his eyes and it's like I'm falling. The ground beneath me has disappeared and so have the trees above. Or maybe it's me. I'm not there anymore—I'm somewhere else, somewhere timeless and dark and empty, somewhere lonely and hopeless and cold, so cold.

There's a flash of light and a pain as sharp as a hot wire slicing through my head.

I scream, or perhaps I just think I do. My body jolts and my head slams backward into the ground.

Saul lets go of my face and moves away.

"That'll do," he says. "Forty-five years. That'll do nicely. Good-bye, Sarah."

I hear leaves scrunching, gravel scraping, but I don't watch him go. Any energy I had left has gone. I lie where he left me, face flopped against cold, wet leaves. The baby's lying beside me. I can see the top of her head, her little nose, her eyes, shut as though she were asleep. But she's not asleep. She's making a noise. Not crying now, but gently testing out what her mouth and lungs can do.

"Hello," I say.

At the sound of my voice, she stops making her noise. She turns her head in my direction and then moves it from side to side. She's searching for me. She must be hungry.

I wish I had the strength to gather her into me. But I don't. Saul's taken every scrap. She won't get any milk from me. It hits me then. I'm going to die. I thought I might the moment I saw Saul's knife, but now I know it. He's taken my life. And if I die, the baby will die, too.

It's so sad, so desperately sad, but there's nothing I can do now. Except soothe her the only way I can. My breathing is fast and shallow, but I try and draw in some air and I sing to her.

"Twinkle, twinkle, little star." My voice is hardly there, but the baby is quiet now. I like to think that she's listening. I sing and I watch her for as long as I can, taking in every little detail, and then, as the last of my strength saps away, I close my eyes and keep singing.

My voice is tiny, a whisper, an echo, and then it's not there at all. The words are still in my head. I follow them with my mind and they get louder again. But it's not my voice, it's someone else's.

"Upper buv the wowd so high . . ."

What a beautiful thing. My baby's learnt to sing. Perhaps she's an angel. Perhaps she was sent to take me away from here.

I want to see her again. Just one more time.

I force my eyes open. There are two little faces in front of me. Two angels. Only one of them is singing.

"Like a diemond in de sky . . ."

"Mia."

She stops.

"A baybee. Baby twinkle, Mummy," she says. She's crouched down in the leaf mold next to the baby and she's got her arm around her.

"Yes, Mia. This is our new baby. Your sister."

My eyelids are sagging. I'd do anything to stay awake. Anything. But it's too late.

"Mummy tired," Mia says.

"Yes," I murmur. "So tired. I love you, Mia. I love you and I love your sister."

Mia leans over and rests her other arm on my leg. Then she lifts her hand up. It's bright red.

"Mummy poorly," she says.

I don't want to frighten her.

"Just tired, darling. I'm going to have a little sleep now. I love you, darling."

"Love you."

She leans in again and kisses me.

My eyes close. Then she does that thing, the thing that Saul did. She opens my right eye with her thumb. She used to do that sometimes when I was asleep in the morning and she wanted me to play with her. It drove me mad, but now we stare eye to eye and I know it's the last I'll see of her and it's so bitter-sweet it hurts. Bitter because this is good-bye. Sweet because if I could have chosen anyone to spend my last moment with, it would have been Mia.

"Mummy poorly," she says again.

Her eyes are the bluest blue, just like mine. Adam used to say he could lose himself in that blue, and now I lose myself in Mia. The last thing I see are those deep, deep pools. They send their light through me and it brings pain, too, but it's a beautiful pain, a pain which blocks out everything else. Blue's supposed to be a cold color, but this is a different blue — warm, comforting, hopeful. It radiates through me, into my toes and fingertips, my skin, my heart, my lungs, my mind, and as I look into Mia's eyes, she's bathed in light. A golden glow around her. My golden child.

"Love you, Mummy."

"Love you, Mia."

There's another noise now, something high-pitched and insistent. But it doesn't matter. Nothing matters. I can't hold on any longer.

ADAM

I'm running toward the gate when I hear a voice, reaching out to me through the fog. It's a whoop of triumph, a great cry of victory. And it's coming from the other side of the wall.

I swing around and through the gateway and then I stop. There's a line of dark trees by the entrance and a gravel path leading through them. And by the path, through the trees, there are stones. Tall, flat slabs of standing stone. This is the place. I've stepped into Sarah's picture, her dream.

The noise is louder here and the whooping has turned into words. "Yesssss! Yesssss!"

I don't need to see him to know who it is, but soon I catch my first glimpse of him between the trees. He's running, leaping, dancing, even. I ain't never seen him like this and there's only one reason why he would be. He done it. He done what he set out to do. He stole the number from my baby and now my baby has only got a few hours left to live.

I should leave Saul. I should find Sarah, find our child, but as I watch him capering about I can feel the blood boiling in my veins. He's evil in human flesh. He shouldn't get away with this. He's not going to.

I start running toward him.

He don't see me until I'm close, then he stops. He's laughing.

"Adam," he says, "the proud father!"

Then he sees the look on my face, and he stops. He don't have time to draw his gun, because I'm on him. I slam my head against his nose, hear the crack as I make contact.

He staggers backward, hands up to his face.

"Adam!" he splutters. "Calm down."

But there's no calming me now, 'cause I seen his number. His new number.

07252075.

It's a peaceful death, a warm death full of love and light.

It's Sarah's.

"You bastard!"

I launch myself at him again, but he's ready this time. He dodges away and sets off running away from me. I tear after him. He's not going to get away this time. I'm only steps behind. The anger's giving me speed I didn't know I had. My fingertips are touching his jacket. I try to get hold of him but I'm not quite there. And suddenly he leaps up, one foot on the pedestal of a tomb, then springs across the gap to land his other foot on the bottom of a monument. He wraps his arm around the waist of a stone angel and fumbles at his belt, searching for his gun.

I've got no answer for a gun. All I can do is get to him before he fires. I lunge forward and yank at his ankles with both hands. He's clinging on to the statue with one hand, drawing his revolver with the other. When I heave, his legs come away from their perch and the angel starts to topple. I flinch as the gun goes off. I don't feel nothing, and now I'm throwing myself out of the way as Saul and the statue plummet down toward me. I roll over, spinning across soft grass, hard stone, and grass again. When I stop moving, I lift my head up and peer around.

Saul is lying awkwardly on his side. The angel's fallen across him, pinning him down. One of his legs is sticking out at the sort of angle a leg shouldn't make. The other leg's bleeding from a small dark wound—the place where the bullet from his own gun went in. The gun's lying a few feet away.

"Adam!" Saul yells. "Get this off of me."

I sit up carefully, testing out my arms and legs. I'm OK.

He tries to twist around, but his body will only move so far. He braces himself against the angel, grips it with both hands, and tries to shift it. It don't move.

I get to my feet and take a step toward him.

For a moment he thinks I'm going to help. Then I bend down and pick up his gun. I hold it in both hands, looking at it, feeling its weight.

"You won't do it. You know you won't," he says.

I stretch my arm out so there's a line from my right eye to the barrel of the gun to Saul's forehead. His eyes are fixed on mine. Sarah's number stares at me. My finger tightens on the trigger.

Out of the corner of my eye, I catch a movement. A shadow streaks across the ground and around the back of a grave. I turn my head in time to see the wormy tail disappearing.

Saul's seen it, too.

"Put the gun down and get me out of here," he says. "There's a rat. It's near me. It's on me, Adam. Get me out of here."

He flaps his arms at the dark space where his legs are trapped and for the first time I notice his hands. They're red, like he's wearing scarlet gloves.

"Whose blood is that?" I ask.

"What?" He's still thrashing his arms about. "Get away! What?"

"Whose blood have you got on your hands?"

He stops for a second and looks at his own fingers.

"Mine, you bastard. You broke my nose."

It's true, his nose is bleeding. There's a dark stream dripping down to his mouth and a streak smeared across his face. He's wiped it once, that's all. It doesn't explain his hands.

Another rat trots along the top of the angel's wing and balances on the end, sniffing the foggy air, before clambering down toward Saul.

If they're interested in Saul and his blood, then Sarah needs me more than ever. I could shoot Saul. This time I'd do it. I could kick his head in. But I think there's something worse.

"Rot in hell, Saul," I say. And then I turn and start running away. It takes him a couple of seconds to realize what I'm doing, for it to sink in. Then he starts pleading, gabbling the words out in desperation.

"Adam, Adam, come back, please. Don't leave me here with them. Just move the stone. I'll leave you alone. I'll give Sarah back her number. Adam. Adam!"

I run through the graves as his shouts turn to roars. Shadows scatter to the left and right as I blunder along.

There's another shape up ahead, a lump or a heap on the ground. There are rats there, too, blurring the edges, darting, moving, shifting. Then something else moves. A pale flash, thrashing from side to side, and I look closer. It's not one heap, it's two. By the side of the bigger heap, there's a small one, a tiny bundle. The bundle's making a noise. Oh my God, it's the baby.

It only takes a few seconds before I'm there. Rats shriek as

I crunch them underfoot. I tuck Saul's gun into my waistband, reach down, and scoop the baby up. She's crying and her eyes are tight shut. There's nothing in the world I want to do more than look at my daughter now, stare at her, take her in, but I'm drawn to the other heap on the ground.

Sarah.

Her skin is as pale as the marble slabs around her. Her eyes are closed. There are rats swarming on her legs. I sweep them away with my feet. They come back for more, but I kick at them and stamp on them until at last they thin out. I crouch down.

"Sarah."

I know she's got Saul's number. 02162029. Am I too late to even say good-bye?

My eyes run down over her body. Her legs are covered in blood. I keep hold of the baby and take Sarah's hand in mine. It's wet. I turn it over and flinch at the vivid red lines across the palms, the flaps of skin on either side. She's been cut with a knife. Someone's cut her.

"He did it," I say to myself. "He did this to you." Saul's roars are still ringing around the place and I think, *Whatever's happening to him right now, it ain't enough.*

Her hand is cold, but not stone-cold, and I feel a flutter of hope. I lean in closer to her and hold my hand just in front of her open mouth.

She's breathing.

"Sarah? Sarah? It's me. Adam. Can you hear me?"

Her eyes flicker open. She's alive, but I can hardly bear to look. I don't want to see it. Death in her eyes.

Then my stomach flips and I stare and stare.

02202054.

She ain't got Saul's number. She's got Mia's.

SARAH

I open my eyes and he's there. It's Adam, but it's Adam like I've never seen him before. There's a light around him, red and gold. I close my eyes and open them again. It's the same. I don't understand.

He's kneeling next to me, holding the baby. Mia was bathed in gold light and now the baby's lying in a twinkling silver-white glow, so bright its purity almost hurts my eyes. Adam's staring at me like he's never seen me before.

"Sarah . . . ," he says. "You're alive. Thank God." He's frowning, though, searching my eyes.

"What is it? What's wrong?"

"Nothing. I'll tell you later."

His eyes are locked on mine, confused. Can he see these colors, too? Has someone flicked a switch somewhere and flushed the world through with light?

"What color am I?" I say.

"What?"

"I can see your colors now. You're red and gold, like your nan always said. Like Mia's drawing. What color am I?"

"I dunno. I can't see 'em."

It's me. Something's changed in me, my mind, my eyes. And then I realize. Saul looked into my eyes, took my number, and gave me his. 02162029 — it flashed through my mind as he ripped my life out of me. And Mia looked again and took his. So that must mean . . . I've got hers. And everything that comes with it. I'm looking at the world through her eyes, through Val's eyes.

"I've got their number, haven't I, Adam: Val's and Mia's? That's what you can see, isn't it? Isn't it?"

He presses his lips together. He hates to tell, always has.

"It's OK. You don't need to say it. I know. 02202054."

For a moment, I think he's going to cry.

Then something moves on my leg, something scratchy, tickly. I jerk it instinctively. Adam wheels around and hits out.

"What is it?" I say.

"Don't worry," he says. "It's gone."

"What has?" But he won't answer me.

I try to prop myself up on my elbows. Not far away someone's shouting, filling the air with their noise.

"Can you sit up?" he says.

"I don't know."

He helps me, and I shuffle backward and lean against a gravestone.

The baby's crying in his arms.

"Give her to me," I say. He gently hands her over. She's moving her head to the left and right, mouth open wide. I start to push my top up, getting ready to feed her. "She's hungry. Our daughter's hungry." I look at Adam, expecting some sort of response, a smile, a loving gesture.

"Can you do that standing up?" Adam says. "It'd be better if you could stand."

He's glancing over his shoulder, looking in front of us and behind.

"Not really," I say. "What is it? What's wrong?"

"Nothing. It's alright. Go on."

"Adam, what's that noise?"

He looks at me and his eyes look haunted.

I don't ask again.

I try and get comfortable. The baby knows what to do. She latches on and even here, in a graveyard in the fog, her suckling relaxes me. It's me and her, doing what mothers and babies have done for the whole of time. Her head is covered by my clothes, but her little legs and feet are sticking out. I could look at them forever, but I don't want her getting cold. I wrap my coat around them.

I bet Mia's cold without her blanket. Now that we're settled, she could snuggle in, too. She's here somewhere. She was singing to me before I went to sleep. Before she gave me her number.

My mind had stopped at the realization that I've got Val's number. It was so astonishing, I didn't take the next step. But

I do now. If Mia gave me her number, then what number has she got?

I start to shiver violently. She must have Saul's.

I look up. Adam's got a huge branch in his hands. He's sweeping it across the ground in big semicircles. Animals scatter in all directions as the brushy twigs reach toward them. Rats.

But there's no sign of Mia anywhere.

Adam turns to look at me and the baby and we both speak at the same time, our mouths mirroring each other's.

"Where's Mia?"

ADAM

I leave Sarah the branch to defend herself with and I start running. Mia could be anywhere, but I'm drawn toward Saul. He's still roaring and it sounds like the noise I heard every time I looked in his eyes, before today. It sounds like 02162029. But he's changed. He's got a number that should never be his. He's not dying . . . is he?

I get nearer and the noise goes quieter. I can still hear him, but his voice is softer, whining, pleading. He's talking to someone.

I speed up, dodging and weaving, trying to find the

quickest route. And then I see him. He's where I left him, but he's not alone. Mia's next to him, squatting down. She's touching his face. He's touching hers. Around them, the ground is black with rats.

"All I need to do is make contact, like this, look into your eyes and reach inside."

"No! No, Mia, get away! Get away from him!"

Still touching Saul, Mia twists around.

"Daddee!"

She leaves Saul and starts running toward me, as waves of rats fan out from her feet. I hurtle toward her, but just before I get to her, she slips on a slimy stone and falls, scraping her knee. She starts to howl, but it's nothing compared to Saul's noise now. His roar could split the sky. It fills my ears, blotting out every other sound. My head's soaked in noise—it's making me deaf, disconnected. I'm seeing everything like I wasn't there, like this was happening to someone else. I'm watching the action unfold on a screen.

I reach Mia and she looks up at me from the ground. There's tears all over her face, her cheeks are streaked with blood and dirt—she's a picture of distress. But her number tells me something else. It's all about happy endings, warmth, and love.

07252075.

She's got Sarah's number. She must have grabbed it back from Saul. So Saul's got . . . ?

"Come here! Come back!" Saul bellows.

I look beyond Mia to where he's writhing on the ground, reaching out toward us, fingers grasping at nothing. He stops squirming and looks at me.

"Adam."

He's not shouting anymore, but I can still hear the sound in my head. It's echoing around and around as his number shocks me over and over again, like an electric fence plugged into my brain. He's got it, the number he had when I met him, the number he tried to get rid of. It's come back to him.

02162029.

"Adam! Adam! Get me out of here! These things, they're eating me alive! Help me!"

"I can't do it, Saul," I say.

"Of course you can. I can't get any leverage, but you can. You can lift it enough for me to —" He stops and his face changes. "You mean you *won't* do it, don't you? But you have to, Adam. The girl's tricked me. She gave the sixteenth back to me. I need to get out, I need to . . ."

"You need to take my number or hers. It's not going to happen, Saul."

"Not yours. Not yours, Adam. I wouldn't do that to you. There are hundreds of people back there. Help me find a good number, then I'll leave you alone. You'll be free to go. No one following you, no one on your tail. I promise. I promise, Adam."

I bend down and pick up Mia. I wipe her tears with my thumb. She wraps her arms around my neck and her legs around my middle. I don't think anyone's ever held me that tight before.

"It's alright," I say to her. "Let's go and find Mum, shall we?"

I look at Saul one last time. There's a rat crawling over his face.

"Adam, come back, I won't touch you. I won't hurt you. I'd never hurt you. We can help each other. Don't leave me here. Adam, don't leave me. Adam, please. Please! PLEASE!"

I turn around and I start running.

"You're killing me, Adam. You're a murderer!"

"No, Saul," I shout as I run, "I'm letting someone else live!"

He unleashes his animal roar. It's the sound of reality catching up with him. No one's gonna rescue him. I've seen it. I've felt it. And now it's coming true. Two hundred and fifty years coming to an end. It tears at me with every step, but it don't pull me back.

Saul—his twisted views, his cruel, selfish, everlasting life—belongs in the past.

I've got one daughter in my arms, another taking her first breaths on earth, and a girl I've loved since the moment I saw her. Saul knew nothing about love, or if he ever did, he forgot it. I won't make his mistakes.

I'm running toward the future.

•   •   •

Red and gold, coming toward me through the stones. The colors of fire. Mia's golden flame merges with Adam's. He may not be her biological dad, but they blend together. They look like they belong. And, thank God, they belong to me.

"Mia!" I cry.

Her pale face is smudged with mud. She's clinging to Adam as if her life depended on it.

"Are you all right, sweetheart? Come here."

She won't let go of him. Won't, can't speak. Her eyes are open, glassy, traumatized.

What on earth has she been through? What has she seen?

"Where did you find her?"

He puts his hand on the side of her head, holding her closer, covering her ear.

"With Saul," he says quietly.

"What happened?"

He shakes his head.

"Later," he says. "We'll talk later."

"But her number, Adam. What about her number?"

"It's alright," he says. "Her number's good now."

The roaring cries in the fog go up a pitch, turning into piercing screams.

"That's him, isn't it?" I tip my head toward the noise.

"It'll stop soon," he says. He closes his eyes briefly and I know what he's thinking. *Please stop now. Make the noise stop.*

But a few minutes later, the silence is almost worse than the screams. It sits heavily in the fog, clinging to the branches above our heads, the wet leaves on the ground.

And I know without a shadow of a doubt. In the end he couldn't escape his number.

It came back to him.

Mia brought it back.

· · ·

For a while the only sound is the rustle of rats. Adam keeps them away — stamping, kicking, sweeping the branch around. Then we hear the buzz of a drone overhead. We're sitting ducks, at least Mia and Adam are, with their silicon Judases lodged under their skin. But it's not uniformed soldiers we see emerging through the fog — it's ordinary folk armed with pieces of wood or bits of railing or not armed at all. Their auras merge together in a rainbow haze. They're dazzling.

Adam draws Saul's gun when we first see them, but he soon puts it away. There's a whole crowd of them, women as well as men.

The guy at the front isn't carrying any weapons and his pale blue eyes light up when he sees the four of us. His color is blue, too. It brings me calmness and confidence before he's even spoken.

"You found them, then," he says to Adam.

"Yeah," Adam says. "This is Sarah, and Mia. And this is our daughter."

The man crouches down.

"I'm Simon," he says to me. "If you can walk, I'd like to take you back to the abbey. We have food there, and shelter. It'll be safer for you all."

One of the women comes forward. She's brought cotton sheets, towels, and clean clothes, and a soothing green presence. She tells me she's a midwife, Alona, and she ushers the others, including Simon, away. She helps me get cleaned up, wraps bandages around my cut hands, wipes the blood and muck off the baby, then wraps her tightly in a sheet, so that only her little face is showing. I beckon her nearer.

"The baby," I say, "she hasn't got . . ." I glance at Adam. He's looking after Mia and talking with Simon. I lower my voice. "She hasn't got any eyes."

Alona frowns.

"Have you seen a baby like this before?" I ask.

She shakes her head. "No, but I've heard about cases. It's a developmental thing, but the child can be perfectly healthy otherwise." She puts a hand on my shoulder. "All her vital signs are very good. She's a beautiful girl." And she is. Her face is like a little apple. Her silver-white light nearly takes my breath away.

Alona helps me to my feet. I'm wobbly but I'm able to walk slowly. I carry the baby and Adam carries Mia. Up close, I can see that her light is flecked with tiny dark spots, scorch marks in her golden flame.

When we get nearer to the gate, Adam moves around to the other side and puts his arm around me.

"Don't look," he says, but it's too late. I've already seen the mass of rats, tattered flesh, and bare bone that is all that's left of Saul.

We leave the graveyard the way we came in and turn into the cobbled street. As we walk, I'm remembering the sea of filth outside the abbey. Everyone's being so kind, I don't know how to say I don't want to camp there, but when we turn the corner into the abbey square, I don't see dirt and rubbish; I see people in all their rich, colorful variety. My spirits soar. My eyes have been opened to the world—I feel like I'm seeing it how it should be seen.

We're ushered inside the church. As we go through the big studded door, a ripple of applause breaks out in the crowd behind us. It builds and builds. No cheering, no shouting or whooping, just hundreds of people clapping.

"What's that for?" I ask.

"It's for us," Adam says. He's not uncomfortable with it, he's smiling. He turns back briefly and waves to the crowd. Then we go inside. We're not the only ones here. It's almost like a hospital—the place is full of the very young, the very old, and the ill. Half the windows are missing and not all the walls are intact, but it's a beautiful space. It's busy here, but there's an overriding sense of calm.

We're taken to a smaller place within the church—a chapel, I suppose. People bustle around fetching bedding and blankets, and soon we've got a sort of nest, away from every-one else. Someone brings us hot tea and then, even more wonderfully, they leave us alone. No fuss, no bother. The four of us cuddle up under a duvet, Mia still clinging to Adam, the baby in my arms.

"Adam," I say. "I need to tell you something."

"And I've got so much to tell you," he says, "I'm almost bursting. I gotta do something first, though. I don't want to, but I've got to."

He's nervous now, pressing his lips together, eyes blinking fast.

"What is it?"

He doesn't answer, but leans over and tickles the baby's face, gently teasing her round, peachy cheek. Her face twitches in response and she moves her head against his finger. She's awake.

"What are you doing?" I ask, but inside me I know.

"Trying to wake her up. I need to see . . . I need to see her number. I don't wanna but I know I got to."

He glances up at me, wanting me to encourage him, and his face changes as he sees mine. He's frowning now. I have to tell him.

"She is awake, Adam," I say. "She just can't open her eyes."

"What?"

"She hasn't got any eyes. That's why Saul didn't take her number. He couldn't."

The frown deepens. He furrows his brow and I can't tell what's going on with him. Anger? Disgust?

He stares at our baby's face.

"Adam, don't hate her. She's still our daughter. It's not a bad thing—it saved her life."

He won't look at me now, he's still staring at her.

"Don't hate her."

Then he runs his thumb gently across the place where her eyes should be. The frown eases away. His face relaxes.

"I'll never know," he murmurs. "I won't know her number."

"Just like the rest of us," I say. "Not knowing."

"Like the rest of you," he echoes. "I can look at her and I'm the same. I don't know the end. All I know is we've got today."

"Is that OK? Are you OK with her?"

"'Course. 'Course I am," he says. "I don't hate her, Sarah. I could never, never hate her. She'll have it tough, though, won't she? It's a tough old world. But at least she don't have to bear the gifts Saul thought she'd have."

"Yes, perhaps that's a blessing. She'll grow up loved, Adam. That's all she needs."

"I wanna hold her," he says. "Mia, shall we hold the baby?"

Mia still hasn't said a word. She's stayed in Adam's arms, curled up, silent. I look at her, wondering what will bring her back to us, and I realize that the black spots in her golden glow are bigger. They've stretched out, spreading like stains.

"Mia, I want you. Come here."

She pouts and looks at me from the corner of her eye. She unwinds a little and lets Adam sit her down next to me. I put my arm around her little shoulders.

"It's all right now, Mia," I say. "We're safe."

Adam takes the baby from me and holds her close. She snuggles in and they look so content together. I can't help thinking Adam's right. England's a harsh place now. Are we really safe? What on earth does the future hold for us? I shut those thoughts away, kiss Mia's curly hair, and bask in this moment, this peace, this intimacy. Here. Now.

· · ·

"Adam," I say later, "we could call her Gemma. Not the same as your mum, but similar, a little tribute. Only if you think it's OK. We could call her something else if you . . ."

"Gemma," he repeats. "Gemma. That's beautiful."

Then he looks at me with tears in his eyes. "Thank you, Sarah. For everything. For Gemma. For Mia."

"You don't need to thank me."

"Yeah, I do. I haven't said things in the past and I regret it. Some things need saying. I love you, Sarah."

"I love you, too."

Mia's restless beside me. I look down at her profile. Her lips are moving, but I can't hear what she's saying. I lean nearer.

"Don' leave me," she murmurs.

"What's that, sweetheart?"

"Don' leave me."

I kiss her face and hold her close.

"We won't leave you. We'll never leave you again. You're safe now. Everything's OK."

I rock her gently, singing under my breath. After a few minutes, her breathing has gone heavier, more even. I think she's falling asleep, but when I peer down at her face, her eyes are wide open. She looks like she'll never close them again.

ADAM

Sarah whispers to me.

"I'm worried about Mia."

They're cuddled up together, but Mia's not asleep. She's staring at nothing, her skin pale, her pupils wide. She looks like a little ghost.

"She'll be fine," I say, but they're empty words. She's seen things a two-year-old shouldn't see. She's done things no one should do. I feel that thing again—a shiver of fear. She's a little girl now, but she won't always be little. What's her life going to be like? How the hell is she going to cope with this? How are we going to cope with her?

"Do you think she knows what she did?" I ask.

"How can she?" Sarah says. "She's only two. It must have been instinct. She could see I was in a bad way and did what she could to help me."

"And Saul?"

"Maybe she thought she was helping Saul, too. He was shouting for help, I could hear him."

I'd like to think this makes sense—and maybe it does.

Mia's such a generous girl. Her instinct is to help.

I'd like to think it, because it's way more comfortable than the alternative. That at some level she knew Saul's number was bad and she gave it back to him to save her own skin. Is that what really happened? Did she beat him at his own game? The thought of it chills my bones.

"How the hell do we deal with this? A girl who can change her fate? Change other people's?"

"Maybe there are two of us," Sarah says quietly. "I've changed twice now."

"Shit. Would you . . . could you . . . ?"

"I don't know. It doesn't seem like something I did. It was like something that was done to me. I don't know if I could."

"What did it feel like?"

She breathes out, like she's forcing all the air out of her lungs—a long breath, almost a sigh.

"I only realized what was going on just before it happened. I feel so stupid, as if I've been going around with my eyes closed. The baby was no good to him. He dumped her and came after me. He was desperate then. He needed a new number and so he took mine. He got close to me, really close. I tried to look away but he forced my eye open and it felt like he put a hot wire into my soul. It was painful, physically painful. He was taking something from me, ripping it out of me. He was taking my life away."

"Sarah —"

"I just felt what I was losing. All my energy, my will to

live—he took it. And in that last second I saw his number, felt it. 02162029." She closes her eyes, shuts them tight, and when she opens them again her pupils are wide and there's shock and fear in them. "I saw his death date, Adam, the number he was giving to me. I saw Mia's, too, when she gave it to me. I understand now, what you see every day."

She twists around and puts her hand up to my cheek and there's something so tender about it. It's not pity—she knows how I feel now. She's felt it, too.

"He took my life away, but Mia gave it back. She gave me her life, her number. She saved me, Adam."

Mia's still awake, her blonde curls framing her face, her eyes blue and wide. She looks like an angel. And that's what she is. She was Sarah's guardian angel and she was Saul's angel of death.

"We have to be so careful with her," I say. "Bring her up right, whatever right is. If only Mum was alive, or Nan. If only we had some help."

Sarah puts her finger to my lips.

"If only's no good. It's no good, Adam. Your mum and your nan are here, anyway. You and me, Mia and Gemma, we carry them around with us. They're part of us. They're in our hearts and minds and they always will be."

"It's not the same. . . ."

"No, it's not the same, but it's what we've got. When we're stuck, when this all gets too much, we need to look inside. The answers will be there."

She's speaking from the heart. She believes this. We can cope. We can do what we need to do. And listening to her, I'm starting to believe it, too.

•   •   •

I leave Sarah tucked up in her nest with the kids. I feel like my eyes are open, really open. The last time I felt like this was just before the Chaos. I knew back then I had to try and help people, get them out of London. But since then I been sticking my head in the sand, denying who I am, hoping the world would leave me alone. I can't do that no more. I'm not sure what I can do, but I know where to start. I gotta find Daniel.

I walk through the abbey and out into the yard. People notice me. Some of them try to shake my hand as I pass. I don't blank them or pretend I haven't noticed. I don't look at the floor. When they call out to me, I stop, take the hand that's offered, look them in the eye. I spend a moment with them, whatever their number's telling me.

"Where are you going?" someone asks me.

"I'm heading back to the bunker," I say. "I need to find my friend, the one who rescued me."

People gather round. I recognize some of them from the graveyard. They want to come, too. And instead of shrugging them off, I accept their help. So we walk together through the streets, past the heaps of rubble and tents and looted shops, and up toward the hill. Overhead, a drone tracks our progress.

"Did you know about the bunker?" I ask.

"We knew. It was a badly kept secret. That's where half our

supplies come from. Black market. And when people disappeared, the rumor is that's where they were taken."

"Did people often disappear?"

"If they started organizing things, making a fuss, making trouble. If they were different. They were picked out. One
minute they were there, the next they weren't."

The shouts in the night, the blood streaked on the walls.
How many, I wonder?

"Look!"

We're at the bottom of the grassy slope now and there are
people coming down the hill toward us. A straggly line of the
walking wounded. One of the group with me gives a shout of
recognition and starts running up the hill. When he reaches
his man, they fling their arms around each other, holding
tight without a word before they break into backslapping and
excited conversation.

"The disappeared are coming back," I say.

I scan the faces coming toward me. Many are bruised
or cut. Some people are limping, walking in twos or threes,
supporting each other. Some are slow, confused. Others are
wildly happy, birds set free from their cage. All of them are met
with kind words and helping hands and shown the way to the
abbey.

The steady stream of refugees keeps on coming and I realize there's no way I'll be able to get into the bunker. Not until
everyone who wants to has got out. All I can do is wait, so I
walk up to the exit in the brambles and I join the welcoming

committee, shaking hands, directing people down the hill. The last one out is Daniel.

His face lights up when he sees me.

"Adam, you've got to move away. We're in at the main entrance—we're going for the communications center. It'll go up any minute now. You've got to move away. Move away!" he shouts to anyone within earshot.

People near us start running and we set off, too. We've only gone fifty feet or so when there's a massive explosion. Everyone on the hill drops to the ground as dust and bits of rock shoot out of the tunnel over our heads. Daniel and I hit the deck. I curl up and tuck my head in as debris starts raining down. There's a crash ten feet away from us. I wince, try to make myself smaller, and wait for the noise to subside.

When I look up, there's a drone lying on the ground next to us.

"They got it," Dan says, uncurling, too. "They blew up command control. No more drones, no scanners, nothing to keep track of us."

We sit up. Below us, the line of people is picking itself up. As people look back up the hill and start to realize what's happened, they high-five each other, start whooping and hollering. I help Dan onto his feet.

"Where's Sarah?" he says. "Is she OK?"

"Yeah, she's fine. She had the baby, a little girl."

He breaks into a broad grin.

"Congratulations," he says. "And Saul, what happened to him?"

"He's gone. He . . ." I'm struggling to choose my words. "He had a nasty accident."

Dan's grin gets broader and then he tips his head back and lets out a "Yee-hawww!" his voice joining the weird and wonderful chorus on the hill. I wait for him to draw breath.

"I gotta ask you, are Marty and Luke really OK? I know what you said to Sarah, but . . ."

He's still grinning.

"Yeah, mate, they're fine. I'll get Carrie to bring them here."

"Sooner the better."

"Of course."

"Are you staying here?" I ask.

"It's as good a place as any," he says. "We've got rid of the cancer; it's time to help the body to heal. We can start here."

"I want to help," I say.

"I was hoping you'd say that."

"Not the way they wanted. I don't want to choose who to help and who to leave. I'm sick of thinking about death. I want to help everyone. I want to help people to live."

He claps his good arm around my shoulders and we start walking toward the city.

• • •

Gemma's crying. She doesn't need changing. She doesn't want to nurse. She jerks her head from side to side, rejecting my attempts to soothe her. Her round face is scarlet.

Adam's been away for a while now.

If he was here, perhaps he could calm her down — I don't seem to be able to help her. I wriggle out of our nest and walk around the chapel. Mia stays put. She's staring ahead blankly, lips moving. The stains on her aura are spreading. You can't see them changing, only notice the difference when you look away and look back.

I bounce Gemma in my arms. My frustration and panic are there in the way I'm moving. I try talking to her gently, and singing, but her cries drown out my voice. I should be able to do this. I coped with Mia on my own, didn't I? I'm sweating and uncomfortable. The day's taking its toll now.

"She's noisy, isn't she?" I say to Mia. She doesn't react. Her aura is a mottled mess of gold and black.

Simon pops his head around the archway.

"Everything all right?"

"She's just crying."

"Can I help?"

"You can try."

He takes Gemma from me. I stand and watch, scraping my damp hair off my forehead. She hasn't even noticed the change. Her face is twisted up, red, angry.

"What about her sister?"

"No, don't. She's . . . she's still in shock."

"Maybe this will help."

"No, really. Leave her. A crying little sister's no fun to hold. Better to wait until she's quiet."

"Of course . . ." He hands Gemma back to me. "I'll get Alona. She's good with newborns."

I resume my pacing, watching Mia at the same time. She's stuck somewhere. I'm sure she's not really here. Her lips are moving again, but soundlessly, mumbling something only she can hear. Wherever she is, it's a bad place. I desperately want, I need, to bring her back.

"Mia," I say. "Will you hold her?"

She doesn't seem to have heard.

I kneel down next to her.

"Mia," I say again, "do you want to hold your sister?"

Her eyes flick to mine. The aura around her head is inky black. A black halo. Her pupils are huge, like they contain a world of pain. And suddenly, I'm really scared. There's something wrong with her. Very, very wrong.

"Hold your hands out," I say firmly.

She obeys me, but like a robot.

I gently place Gemma in Mia's arms, putting my hands underneath, cradling them both.

This time, Gemma notices the change. She's still crying, but she turns her face toward her sister. Mia stares at her, but

not with the vacant stare that's been rattling me — she's looking, examining her sister's face.

"Baby wake up," she says.

"She is awake, Mia. She hasn't got eyes like you and me.
She's got sleepy eyes. She can hear you, though. You can talk
to her."

"Hello, baby," Mia says.

Gemma stops crying. Mia pokes at her face.

"No, not like that, Mia. Give her your finger to hold.
Here . . ."

I move Mia's hand so that it makes contact with Gemma's
little fist. The moment the two touch, Gemma unwinds her
fingers and grips onto Mia's. Mia looks up at me and smiles.

"Baby hold on," she says.

"She likes you," I say. "You're her big sister. Can you sing to
her? She'll like that."

"Do 'Twinkle,'" Mia says.

"You do it. She wants to hear your voice. I'll help."

We start singing, but soon my voice fades and stops.

Mia's aura is changing before my eyes. Where the girls
are holding hands, their colors blend. Mia's is becoming
gold again. Pure gold. Gemma's sparkling light is moving up
her arm, bleaching away the black stains.

Mia glances up at me.

"Keep going, sweetie. She loves it."

There's noise drifting in from outside, a buzz of excitement rippling through the church. But I'm not going anywhere. I'm transfixed by what's going on with my two girls.

Adam clatters into the chapel, with Daniel in tow. Daniel's hand is wrapped up but they're both in high spirits, arms around each other's shoulders.

"How are my girls?" Adam says.

Mia looks up and beams.

"They're fine," I say. "Adam, something amazing's happened." I leave the girls sitting together and run over to him. He lets go of Daniel. "Mia's aura was marked"—I keep my voice low—"but I think Gemma's cleaned it. When she touched her, the darkness started to go. Mia's gold again. Pure, shining gold. I can't believe it."

Adam puts his arm around me, pulling me in. "So Gemma's got her own gift," he says, and a smile plays at the corners of his mouth. "I thought we'd have to look out for her all the time."

"Adam, her blindness saved her. Maybe she's the most special of us all—"

I stop sharply. Hate the thought that's come into my head. "What?"

I don't know how to say it, but I know I have to ask.

"Is Gemma safe with her sister? Has Mia's number changed? What if she's so powerful she doesn't need to see Gemma's eyes to take her number?"

I have to know. Saul's aura was black and it tainted Mia's. Could she end up like him?

Adam looks at the girls.

"Mia," he says. "Look at Daddy. Are you singing to Gemma? Did you make her stop crying?"

Mia looks up. Her eyes are shiny with excitement.

"Baby like 'Twinkle,'" she says. "Shh, baby."

"That's right. Good girl."

He turns back to me.

"It's alright. Her number's the same."

"She's still got mine?"

"Yeah. Do you mind?" he says, looking down at me and pulling me close again. I can feel his heart pounding in his chest.

"It's a good number, isn't it?" I say. He looks pained. "You don't have to answer. I saw it in your notebook, before the Chaos."

"It's the best number I've ever seen," he says quietly. He holds me closer and for a moment it feels like it's just me and him here, no one else, not even the children. His mouth is next to my ear. I close my eyes and he whispers to me. "It's bathed in love and light. If she keeps it, slipping out of this life will be so calm for her, Sarah, so peaceful. It's the most beautiful end anyone could have."

I open my eyes and tilt my head so I can see him. His eyes are closed but a tear squeezes through his lashes and trickles down his face.

"What's wrong?" I say. "I couldn't ask for anything better for her."

His eyes flick open and more tears spill out. There's anguish all over his face.

"It's your number, Sarah. It should be yours."

I wipe his tears away with my fingers, then cup his face with my hands.

"No," I say. "This is the way it should be. We'll raise our family the best way we can, we'll surround them with love. We'll teach Mia to hold on to her number and Gemma can use her gifts to heal. She hasn't got eyes, but just think what Gemma might help us see. Who knows, our girls might have something to teach all of us. Whatever happens to you and me, there's a happy ending waiting for both of them. There has to be."

I turn away from Adam and look back at the girls.

Mia's head is bathed in gold again. The only black spots are around her legs and they're dissolving as I watch. Mia leans forward and lays her cheek against Gemma's and the last pinpoints disappear.

CHILDREN ON THE BEACH

The girl sits on the beach. She draws pictures in the sand with her finger while the others run and chase in the evening sunshine.

Marty and Luke are playing with Gemma, taking turns to swing her around. She staggers, giggling, between the two of them.

"Careful. Not too much!" Her mum's voice carries across the beach from the sand dune.

"That's enough!" her dad shouts.

The girl twists around to look at them, standing with their arms around each other. Behind them she can just see the patched-up roofs of the cottages and the bare rafters of the new houses being built. It's been a long day but a good one. When lots of people work together, a house can grow from nothing in a few hours. Her dad's good at getting people to work together. That's why they've moved around so much. People like it when he visits.

But she's tired of traveling. She wants to stay put, have a home, somewhere they can all live together forever and ever.

She looks back at her drawing in the sand—a house and six people and a big sunshine in the sky above—and she traces some words underneath: *HAPY EVA AFTA.*

She hears the boys' raucous laughter. Gemma's truly dizzy

now. She stumbles to one side, tries to right herself, and careers off the other way.

The girl calls out to her. "Gem, come here! Gem, this way!"

Gemma turns toward her and smiles.

"Come here!"

Gemma weaves her way unevenly across the sand, as the girl guides her in with her voice. When she's a couple of feet away, she launches herself forward toward the girl, diving through the air, arms held wide. The girl catches her and they tumble backward in a heap of arms and legs.

"Gemma, you big lump! What would you do if I didn't catch you?"

Gemma flings her head back and laughs, then she moves her hands up to the girl's face, tracing the creases at the corner of her mouth, the laughter lines by her eyes.

"Mia," she says. "My Mia." And she kisses her full on the lips.

The girl wipes the saliva away.

"Eugh, Gemma, that was a wet one," she says. "Shall we find Mum and Dad?"

"Yes."

They disentangle themselves and stand up, holding hands.

The boys are miles away now, running toward the distant sea.

Mia and Gemma turn toward the dunes and set off walking. Their long shadows streak across the rippled surface of the sand, joined at the hand like cutout paper dolls.

ACKNOWLEDGMENTS

I would like to thank everyone who has supported me during the writing of all three *Numbers* books:

David, for pointing me in the direction of the Frome Festival.

The Frome Festival, for encouraging me through their short story competition, and for matchmaking.

Friends and family who have hosted, and encouraged, my writing, especially Mum and Dad, Ann and Peter in Spain, and Ann and Dave in Jersey.

Friends who have taken an interest in my writing, especially work friends at Keynsham Town Council and Bath & North East Somerset Council.

Everyone at Chicken House, who have done such a brilliant job, including Barry for all his wheeling and dealing, and especially, this time, Imogen, Rachel Leyshon, and Chrissie.

All the lovely people involved in translating my books and publishing them outside the UK, especially those who have looked after me in various countries — Anja and Hilke in Germany, and Monique and Janetta in the Netherlands — and Elinor for making all this possible.

The wonderful librarians, School Library Service staff, teachers, and journalists I've met who are so busy promoting and celebrating reading.

And finally, the readers, especially those who've written to me or come to see me speak. Your reaction to my books has meant the world to me.